VINCENT G. BIVONA JR.

PLOTS ARISING

BOOK 1

BOOK REVIEWS

This fantasy tale will enthrall, frighten, and devastate you while leaving you utterly captivated by the plot unfolding before you. What makes this story even more exciting is the lively cast of characters which consist of elves, dwarves, and humans alike. The real question is, though, will Dak'tari avenge her beloved by destroying those who betrayed them? One thing is for certain - any fantasy fiction fans out there will be delighted they decided to come along for the ride for this intense epic story full of incredible imagery that will stick with you for ages. Be sure to pick up your copy of Blood of Deception: Plots Arising Book 1 by Vincent G. Bivona today! You will not be disappointed.

- Alyssa Avina, ***Hollywood Book Reviews***

Brilliant with detail and palpitating with suspense, Blood of Deception: Plots Arising delivers a knuckle-hard plotline with an unforgettable set of characters. Vincent G. Bivona does a great job of opening the minds of readers and giving us a story we can fully embrace. Blood of Deception has all the best traits of a dark mystery with a true crime vibe infused with fantasy. If you enjoy books full of intrigue and suspense, this will not disappoint. I highly recommend this book to anyone that likes thrillers, dark fantasies and that will keep you guessing till the very end.

Liz Konkel, ***Pacific Book Review***

Published in the United States of America

ISBN
979-8-88945-236-2 (Paperback)
979-8-88945-237-9 (Hardback)

Brilliant Books Literary
137 Forest Park Lane Thomasville
North Carolina 27360 USA

DEDICATION:

To Stan Smith whose ability to spin a tale
was the inspiration for this story.
And Danna Gibson whose constant harassment
of asking me, have you finished yet?' led me to
believe that maybe I had something.

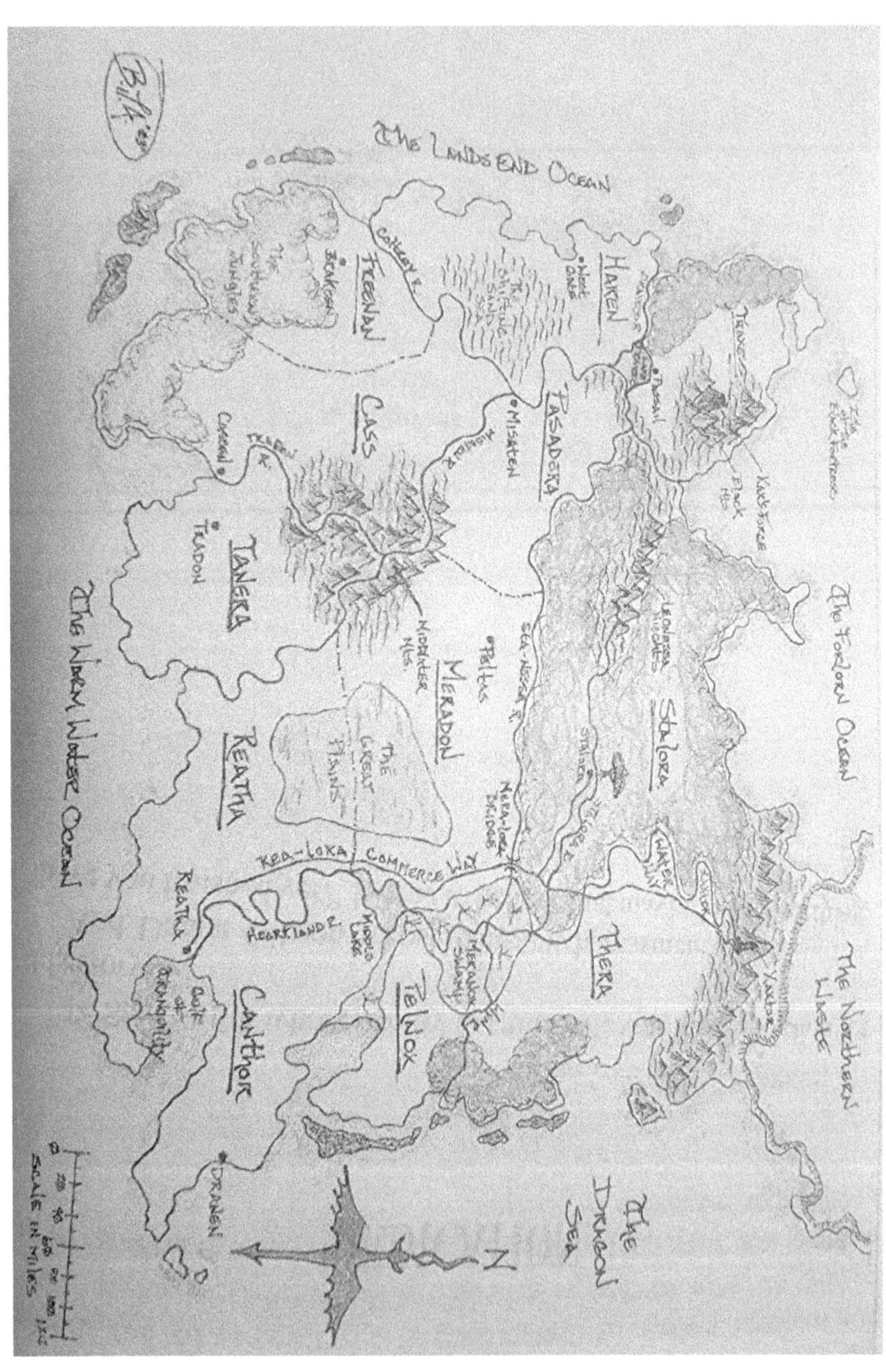

Map by Brett Antoline

PROLOGUE

I

An ear-piercing scream reverberates off the slime-covered, black stone walls from the pregnant women laying in the midst of a pentagram. Five human skulls, one at each point of the star, glare at the pregnant woman like an audience of macabre jack-o-lanterns. The glowing coals inside of each skull emit an eerie orange light from the blankly staring eye-sockets, which instead of illuminating the scene being played out before them, cast it into a ghastly specter of shadows and nightmares.

From out of the shadows a figure steps into the sickly orange light. His movements are the flow of water, sure, steady, and fluid. Stepping towards the woman he makes no sound, disturbing neither dust nor pebble as he makes his way to her side. He is covered completely in black except for a thin dark crimson silk cord the color of clotting blood, tied around his waist. His eyes, hidden in shadow, are thin slits bound between his tight-fitting hood and mask. Strapped upon his back is a sheath, with the hilt of a katana pointing skyward above his shoulder. Tucked within his belt hangs a sai, with midnight blue runes glowing along its length.

A voice like the grating of stone against stone issues from out the darkness, seemingly from nowhere and everywhere at once. "It's almost time, get ready! You remember our bargain?"

"Of course! What do I want with a child anyway? Even if it is…Well, we both know what it is. You just remember your part." Answers the figure draped in black.

"Remember your place, and who you address *mortal!*" Comes the voice, ire infusing the voice, causing the cavern to quake with his flaring fury.

"I'm sorry Lord." The man says humbling himself before the voice. "I grow impatient, I mean no disrespect. Please forgive me."

"Very well. Just remember who serves whom. I would *almost* regret it if I had to refresh your memory."

The woman screams again, pulling her feet in and raising her knees up and out. She grunts, sits up, and pushes.

From the shadows, the voice booms out. "Now, Do it now!"

The man quickly steps forward and in one smooth motion draws his katana and swiftly severs the woman's head before she even utters one final squeal. Before her torso has a chance to even flop back to the floor he's sheathed his sword, withdrawn his dagger from his boot, and is kneeling next to the headless woman. While the blood still pulses from the stump of her neck he slices open her belly exposing the child within. "What the hell is this?" he exclaims, staring down at the exposed child.

"Problem, my little assassin?" The voice coos.

"It's a bitch! It was supposed to be a son, not a sniveling bitch child!"

The voice erupts in laughter. "What you desired is of no consequence, I desired a female. I've come to realize that a female can be far more devious and pliable than a male. For my needs, a female is perfect."

"There will be problems back at the Black Fortress. Some will not tolerate a female." Replies the man now subdued. "But I do understand what you mean."

"Your understanding means nothing to me! Just your obeisance. And Cantanis will make sure that my desires are carried out despite what your brothers might think."

Nodding in acquiescence the black figure reaches down and removes the baby from the headless body of her mother. As he rises with the child in his arms the light from the skulls dances upon the girls wide staring eyes. "Hmm," he says slightly awed, "she has her mother 's eyes."

II

Lightning cleaves the inky blackness of the storm-filled night, momentarily baring beneath it the black-clad figure making his way up the thin, winding path perched upon the side of the blasted, barren mountain. The wind rips at the figure trying vainly to cast him, and the child he bears, off the path to smash upon the rocks and surf below. The rain ushered on by the storm's fury tears at his clothes and skin, as if it were sand in the sandstorm. The lightning strikes again, accompanied by a tooth rattling explosion of thunder, revealing to the figure his destination. A black fortress set atop the mountain. The black stone fortress sits squarely atop the flat mountain, its top appears to have been hewn away and left smooth by the blade of some long-forgotten gargantuan axeman. Rising eighty-feet into the night sky nothing mars or breaks up its surface. No doors or entrances can be seen. No flags or banners flutter from its flat top. No symbols or inscriptions indicate who or what might reside here. Just a giant, black stone block sitting lost and alone atop the wailing mountain.

The figure approaches a section of the wall, appearing no different from any other section, looking down at the squirming bundle within his arms. Though cold and wet, the baby squirms but at no point does she cry, whimper, or otherwise show her discomfort. Glancing at her, a look almost akin to pride crosses his features. Shifting the child, he frees a hand and seems to etch some sort of design or symbol upon the wall. Silently a crack appears forming a rectangle which opens allowing him access to the Black Fortress.

Stepping through the doorway, which closes of its own accord, he finds himself in a long smooth hallway, with floor tiles the same clotted-blood color as his belt. Extending from the walls about every twenty feet are petrified arms. Clasped within the gnarled hand of each arm is a softly glowing ball casting light upon the hall. At the end of the hall is an archway covered in blazing scarlet runes. Passing through the archway, he enters a large chamber covered in tapestries depicting various acts of violence.

Beheadings, poisonings, disembowelments, strangulations, and every other form of killing was depicted in vivid detail somewhere on those cloth hangings.

Set in the center of the room is a large, crescent-shaped, onyx table around which sits twelve figures dressed as the man who enters carrying the baby. Across from the table, facing the archway sits an ancient figure of a man dressed in black robes, with the loose-fitting hood draped upon his frail-looking shoulders. The throne, which supports his ancient backside, are the gold-dipped skulls of his most prized trophies. Kings, queens, generals, heroes, and powerful mages all take a place in cradling his wizened frame.

As the man walks through the archway the old man raises his head. His voice is clear and strong showing no trace that it comes from the throat of someone who appears as old as the mountain upon which they stand.

"Ma'rel my son, you have returned." He speaks as if happy to see Ma'rel, but his eyes contain no joy. Just the cold hardness of death, revealing nothing yet absorbing everything. When his eyes latch upon you they seem to peer past your physical body and bore down into one's s soul, leaving you naked, vulnerable, and exposed. "So is that him?" The ancient one asks.

"In a way." Ma'rel's tone is flat, a simple statement.

The old man's eyes narrow. "What do you mean, 'in a way?"

"The child is not exactly what was planned for." He pauses for a second. "The child is female."

The men around the table instantly explode. "Never!"

"She must die!"

"Kill it now!" All the men around the table erupt in a cacophony of outraged hysteria demanding the death of the child. Standing they start drawing daggers from hidden reservoirs within their clothing. Ma'rel lightly fingers the hilt of his sword above his shoulder adjusting his hold on the child to make it more secure. It was not for the love of the child, he was incapable of love, it was just that he had too much at stake to let the child die now.

A chuckle breaks through the riot of outraged shouts. Immediately a hush falls upon the twelve, as everybody turns to look at the old man as he slowly stops laughing. "Bring the child to me," he orders Ma'rel.

Ma'rel, dropping his hand from his sword's hilt, walks up to the old man. Dropping down to one knee he lifts the child towards the ancient figure. "My child, master," he says, bowing his head.

The old man takes the child and removes the blanket from over its face. "Well, she is quite pretty." He softly whistles. "The eyes though, I guess, are a trait from its mother's side."

One of the figures at the table blurts out in a voice filled with rage. "You cannot allow this!"

The old man's hand is back in his lap before the foolish figure lets out his first scream. His hand rushing to his face is to late do anything other than claw at the shaft of the small dart protruding from his left eye.

The old man's voice is cold and chilling, sending a shiver up the spine of all within the room. "NO ONE tells me what I can do!"

"But master, who will teach the child?" One of the figures asks meekly.

"I will fool! Who else?" States Ma'rel.

"No, I will."

The intake of breath is audible within the room.

"But master, you have not deigned to teach in over two hundred years. Please do not misunderstand, I am honored that you would teach my child. I just... as you wish." Ma'rel stops before he says something to anger his master.

"It's all right. This child is special, she is destined for great things. You know this. And besides, you have other things to do, you will not be around to teach her. Also if she is to be the first female to be trained in our order, it should be I who teaches her. Now all of you get out and take that with you." He flicks a wrist at the man writhing on the floor, desperately trying to remove the dart from his ruined eye." Ma'rel come to my chambers tomorrow so we can go over your next task. Now go get cleaned up." As Ma'rel reaches a passage branching from the chamber the old man asks. "So does the child have a name?"

"Yes, master. I named her Dak'tari."

After the chamber has emptied the old man looks down upon Dak'tari. As a dark voice touches his mind he blanches.

"No, I will teach her. You will prepare her for me, but she is to be mine. She is the one I've been waiting for."

"Yes, my lord." The old man replies reverently to the voice within his head.

III

Dressed in a black silk robe, with a crimson heart dotted with three holes stitched on the back, Ma'rel heads for the old man's chambers. The robe is tied around his waist with the same blood-red colored, silken belt, only this one is wider and longer, extending down to just above the knees. His face is that of someone in their mid-thirties, thin, angular, and hawk-like. His gray eyes are deep-set, constantly moving, seeing everything and missing nothing. Though home and supposedly safe, he's learned that you don't break from a lifetime's worth of training just because you feel safe. Safety is an illusion, which can vanish within the space of a heartbeat. His hair, now loose and flowing down his back, shimmers from the water and orange light caught between the strands, drops a good ten inches past his shoulders. He runs his fingers through it, raking tiny droplets of fiery crystals from his hair. In his left ear he wears a small, whitegold earring, plain unless you were to see the tiny runes etched upon its inner surface. Enchanted with the ability to resist magic, it is one of his most prized possessions. Not so much for what it does but for what he went through to keep it. Retrieved from the head of one of his marks, the High Mage of the wizard's guild for the city of Tradon. After rubbing the ear-ring his hand drops to his side as the memory of that night drifts back to him.

*****

Glancing down, from his perch on the side of the Mage's Tower, he has a spectacular view of the city at night. Lights twinkling in the windows resemble a pitch-black blanket strewn with diamonds that glisten and shine from the light of the moon. The view is that of the gods looking down with contempt and disdain upon the mortals beneath them.

«Is that what you like to think you are?» He sneers. «Gods. Well, tonight a god dies. «

Hearing a noise from the street far below, a small crossbow appears in his hand as if by magic. His eyes peer into the blackness far below, searching for the source of the commotion. Spotting the disturbance, a pair of pathetic ruffians in the process of relieving some poor bastard of his gold and life, Ma›rel turns back to the job before him. Placing the crossbow back in the holster at his side, he continues upward ten feet, to the windowsill which he has been climbing towards. Quickly he reaches it, easing his head up over the ledge as he looks around. Seeing that the room is empty he examines the window ledge itself. Not seeing what he is apparently looking for, he looks back into the room yet again. A smile crosses his face, hidden by his mask, as he spots what he has been searching for. A mirror across the room reflects the red runes which burn in the wall around the window sill.

Looking at the runes reflected in the mirror. Ma›rel realizes that if someone crosses the window sill their soul will become trapped within the mirror, leaving them a mindless, soulless slave to the mage. Reaching into a pouch at his side, Ma›rel removes a small vial. Popping the top with his thumb, he sprinkles the gray dust into the glass-less window. He then begins to move his hand back and forth, starting at the top and working down. The dust remains in place forming what resembles a gray cloudy pane of glass. As the last of the dust solidifies the runes in the room go dark. Placing the empty vial back in his pouch he drops down, holding on to the ledge with both hands. Bringing his feet up, he places them against the wall, pushing off he flips upwards and backward. The dust window shatters as if it was glass, but without sound, and floats off onto the wind turning back into dust. Ma‹rel, landing on his feet as if he was part cat, glances around. Shelves covered in tomes, scrolls, jars filled with potions, herbs, powders, and creature parts line the walls in neatly aligned sections. In the center of the west wall, a fireplace stands cold and full of ash, awaiting for the tender kiss of a spark to re-ignite it. At a large desk covered in arcane papers sits a large, plush leather chair, its back to the fireplace. Two more chairs sit in front of the desk, neither one as large and plush as the one behind the desk. There is no bed or other items of comfort, just a plain large experiment table with flasks, beakers, and burners. Ma‹rel smiles as he realizes that his information was correct, this is the mages work area. Not that he cares about the discomfort inflicted upon his source, matter-of-fact he enjoyed that, but he is glad that he didn't waste his time extracting erroneous information from the novice. The poor apprentice had also said that Pax-Ra would return here after the conclave to continue his research. Ma‹rel wonders if anytime would be spent trying to figure out what happened to one of their numbers. Not that it mattered, shortly they would have greater things to concern themselves about. Ma‹rel moves to the side of a bookshelf behind the backside of the door, where the shadows are deeper than anywhere else in the room. Slipping into the shadow, as if it was water if engulfs him. Where once there was a shadow and a man, now there is only shadow, and now he waits.

After about a half-hour, noise can be heard coming from the opposite side of the door. As the door opens light streams in from the hallway. The door closes, revealing a man in red robes appearing to be in his fifties. He has a short, well-groomed salt and pepper beard that matches his hair. There is a ring on each hand, one with a ruby, the other a piece of amber. In his left ear is a small, white-gold earring.

As Pax-Ra enters the room he speaks a word of command. Instantly the cold ashes in the fireplace ignite as if they were well-cured pine logs.

Pax-Ra turns in alarm as the words «Prepare to die!» are whispered from the shadow of a bookshelf behind him. He spins just in time to see the glimmer of steel slashing towards his neck. Uttering the word that will transport him to another place, the mage stops to wonder why his body is spinning away from his disbelieving eyes. Then he realizes that his spell will never work as his body, spewing blood, collapses next to his wide-eyed head.

As the body stops its flopping the ruby ring explodes in a mass of whirling fireballs. Swirling balls of fire fly around the room, shattering jars and igniting scrolls, tomes, and furniture. Ma›rel flips backward, narrowly missing a screaming ball of fire. The fireball smashes into a row of shelves behind him, lined with jars, sending a hand-size piece of glass to tear a chunk from out of his side.

«Shit!» he whispers, placing a hand against his wounded side.

As the last of the fireballs disperse, Ma›rel bends over to perform his final task before leaving.

In a matter of seconds, mages start materializing within the room, spell components in their hands, and words of power on their lips. But the only thing awaiting them is a wrecked, smoldering room, the ashy remains of a scroll, and the headless body of their leader. His hands laid neatly across his chest, palms up and cupping his skullcap, like an offering plate to some obscene god. His brains, scooped from his skull, sit within the center of the grotesque plate, atop which rests his heart with three neat holes in the form of a triangle puncturing it.

Materializing back at the Black Fortress, The Scarlet Brotherhood keep, he presents his trophy, the emptied head of PaxRa, to the old man. As the old man accepts the head he rolls it within his withered hands. Noticing the earring he removes it, rolls it between two fingers, and examines the runes traced on the inside. Ma›rel can only wait for what he knows is coming next. Remaining on one knee he lowers his head in submission and waits for the blow which is sure to come.

«Rise my son, there's no harm done. You›ve done well. « The old man says while lovingly caressing the hollowed-out head of Pax-Ra. In less time than it takes a flame to flicker, Ma›rel is standing at attention before the old man. As Ma›rel reaches his full height, blinding stars slam into his brain, trying desperately to force him into unconsciousness.

Shouting to himself, «No damn you, don't you dare blackout!» Knowing full well that to lose consciousness would surely mean his death, he rouses himself from the sweet arms of oblivion. Pulling himself back from his near-faint his breath gushes from his lungs, as for the first time his brain has a chance to register what is being done to his body.

Ma›rel stands on his toes, back arched, head and arms thrown back, looking as if he were a life-sized puppet suspended from a stick thrust into his side. For that was pretty much what he was. For if not for the old man s claw-like hand holding him up by the wound in his side he would surely have fallen.

Before Ma›rel had realized it, the old man had stood, stepped forward, and inserted his taloned, skeletal hand into the wound made by the exploding jars.

«So you›re back? Good.» The old man whispers into Ma›rel's ear. «You know why we have our rules, don't you?»

Ma›rel can do nothing more than fluttering his glazed eyes.

«We are never to be mistaken for thieves. Nothing is ever to be taken from a mark. «He speaks to Ma›rel as if he was a father, telling his son to calm down in a crowded marketplace before he breaks something. Not cruelly or harshly, but as though this has been discussed before and will not be discussed again. Clutching Ma›rel's jaw, the yellowed nails of his fingers piercing his cheeks, he forces Ma›rel's eyes to focus and look at him. «If you were not my best disciple, you would be dead now. But if you ever make another mistake you will be dead before you have time to realize you made one. Do we understand each other?»

Somehow Ma›rel finds the ability to produce enough saliva and breath to croak, «Yes master.» The old man releases his hold on Ma›rel who instantly collapses to the floor as if his bones were suddenly turned to jelly. Fighting back the urge to throw up he chooses to concentrate on breathing instead.

As the blue-yellow sparks of star-fire start to dance in front of his eyes due to lack of oxygen, his lungs remember their function. Sucking in large gasping rasps of air, his hands slip on the blood-slick floor. Pushing himself back up, he looks down noticing for the first time the extremely large scarlet pool he is laying in. Remembering the gaping hole in his side, he looks down again at the life fluid seeping from him. Slowly he slips back down like a balloon slowly losing air. Feeling his pulse slow down, as the last of his essence slips away, he starts to drift upon the sweet waves of tranquillity.

Just as he is sure he has passed the point of no return, a voice tears asunder the fog. «Don't you dare die on my floor! Get up now!»

He drags himself up and out of the inky black waters and back onto the gravelly shore. Clawing his way back to the surface and up the unforgiving cliffs of consciousness, he finds himself on his knees before the old man.

The old man is back on his gilded skull-covered throne, holding a small vial of blue liquid. «Now come to me! « He orders, rolling the vial across his knuckles as if it were a coin.

Ma›rel tries to rise to his feet, but the dizzying effects due to the loss of blood cause him to nearly fall back into unconsciousness, and he collapses back into his own blood. Struggling he manages to get back up to his hands and knees. His arms quiver like a moth stuck in a spider's web, his face is the pale color of bleached flour, and from his legs down he feels nothing. He pulls himself the eternal four feet, across the blood-soaked floor, to his master's feet.

When Ma›rel reaches him, the old man gently reaches down and takes him under the chin. «Here drink this. «He says removing the seal with his thumb and pouring the contents down Ma›rel›s throat.

The influx of relief was so intense it almost brought a tear to Ma›rel's eyes. Within four heartbeats warmth returned to his body, casting aside the freezing hands of death. The airflow into his lungs comes in the deep, full belts of euphoria, instead of the last gasps of a man trapped in a collapsed mine. The wounds on his side and cheeks close, leaving a nasty-looking scar on his side and drying rivulets of blood on his face.

As the first signs of relief course through his body, Ma›rel immediately assumes a position of subjugation before the old man. Bowing down, his knees under him and his forehead touching the floor, he says nothing waiting for the old man to dismiss him or instruct him some more.

Ma›rel was not sure how long he knelt there, but it seemed as if it were an eternity. No sound was made, nor anything said, nor did anyone come to talk to the old man. But Ma›rel knew he was there sitting on his throne, doing what, Ma›rel had no idea. Ma›rel stared at the floor, knowing if he moved the slightest muscle the old man would if he was lucky, break his neck and be done with it.

The oppressive, numbing silence that gave one a chance to do nothing but contemplate your errors and make sure they were never made again was finally lifted.

«Rise my son.» Says the old man, the kind, fatherly tone once again in his voice. Ma›rel quickly arises and comes to attention. «I believe you have learned your lesson for today. So you will always remember, you can have this.» He holds up the earring retrieved from Pax-Ra. «Step forward.» He says pulling a dart, with a needle sharp point, from a sleeve.

As Ma›rel steps forward the old man deftly pierces and inserts the ear-ring, with one fluid motion, into Ma›rel's, left ear.

«It will shield you from all but the most powerful of magic. Now go and we shall never speak of this again.» The old man then leans back in his throne and closes his eyes.

*****

Continuing towards the old man's chambers Ma'rel drops his hand from his side, realizing that a lot has happened in ten years.

The hall ends at a solid ebony door, polished to such a high sheen that if not for the scarlet "S" blazing on the door, it would look as if the hall ended in a void. Stopping in front of the door Ma'rel inscribes a "B" on top of the "S". As soon as he closes the "B" the "S" emits one blinding red pulse of energy. The energy pulse swirls around Ma'rel, engulfing him in a crackling, sizzling crimson blanket. The energy field sends a tiny static charge coursing through his body then leaps from him and back into the

"S" on the door. When the last of the energy is absorbed back into the door it silently swings open, allowing him admittance.

As the door opens Ma'rel hears the old man from inside. "Come in Ma'rel."

Ma'rel enters the small room, a twenty-foot square with a petrified arm sconce set in the center of each wall. It stands near empty, except for a solid black stone throne, set beneath the sconce on the far wall where the old man sits, and one other chair.

"Have a seat." The old man indicates the chair across from him. Plush, high-backed and white, it is a strange contrast to the rest of the room. Looking at the chair one would at first think it was made from thin, pale leather. But Ma'rel knew it was made from the sweet skin of virgin elf maids. It was quite pleasing to the touch.

Ma'rel taking a seat waits for the old man to speak.

"So you know what is required of you." The old man finally says eyeing Ma'rel intently.

"Yes, master."

"Remember our lord has been waiting over two-thousand years for his chance to return. If you fail..." He shakes his head as a look of almost sorrowful compassion covers his features. "What I would do to you is nothing compared to what you will endure at the hands of Uthanor. Now go and prepare yourself. You leave in the morning."

CHAPTER 1

THE JOYS OF GROWING UP

I

The four-year-old little girl looks up at the door as it opens. She sits on the cold stone floor, wrapped in a plain black silk robe with a thin white belt tied around her tiny waist. A little, white cotton ball of puppy tugs at one end of her belt, growling in playful frustration.

The walls are bare except for a lighting orb mounted to each wall. In one comer is a small plain bed, really no more than a cot. At the foot of the bed sits a wooden chest that holds her few clothes.

A wooden table and chair make up the rest of the room's sparse decor.

As the old man enters the room, the little girl jumps up, yanking the belt from the puppy's mouth, who barks and yips at its toy being snatched away. Standing straight before the old man she waits for him to speak.

The old man kneels in front of the little girl and takes her little cherub of a face within his gnarled hands. He gently strokes her cheek with a thumb and lifting her face peer into her eyes. Her eyes are a softly-rounded almond shape, much like an elf's. But instead of the purple, gold, or emerald color of the elves, hers are a solid midnight blue, with no iris or pupil breaking up the surface. Instead, hers are infused with a myriad of tiny red flecks, which twinkle like a night sky full of fire diamonds. The seductive and alluring nature of those eyes, even at this young age was interesting to the old man. But what intrigued the old man was the way his gaze was reflected by those dark orbs. Looking as hard as he could he couldn't peer inside her, he couldn't see what she was thinking. This bothered him slightly, but with her parentage was not surprising.

Rising from his knee, the old man runs his fingers through her curly blonde hair. His looks and caresses, though similar to a grandfather's loving caresses upon a favorite granddaughter, were more akin to a doctor examining a special test subject.

"Come Dak'tari," he commands, "It's time you embraced your destiny."

Turning he walks out of the room. Dak'tari, following behind him, stops to close the door and lock the puppy in the room. Dropping a small, dainty hand in front of the puppy's nose, which is half out the door, she starts to shoo him back.

The old man stops and turns back towards Dak'tari and the puppy. The corners of his mouth turn upwards, in the contented smile of a parent watching a child play with a favorite gift received on Yule morning.

The old man had given her the puppy two weeks ago. Before then she had nothing to break up the agonizing monotony of her childhood. She had no friends and no one to play with. There were men around, but they would just ignore her as if she didn't exist. Except for one with a patch over one eye. Who would glare at her with that one good eye as if he wished her dead? And if he ever passed her alone in one of the hallways he would roughly shove her out the way to smack against the wall, cussing her as he passed.

Of course, the old man was there, he brought her food and bathed her. Taught her about various herbs and plants and the ghastly effects they would have upon those that imbibed them. And how to defend herself with flips, dives, kicks, and punches. But other than telling her what was required of her at the moment it was never discussed what she might be feeling or what she might want to do. Not that Dak'tari cared, something about the old man made the little wispy hairs on the back of her neck stand up and quiver. He had never done anything but care for her, but something about his eyes chilled her blood. When he looked at her, she would feel like a bird trapped within the hypnotic gaze of a cobra. She could tell by the way his mouth drew up, like a dying rose bloom, that he didn't see something he was looking for. She wished she knew what it was. Though he was not overly kind, till he got her the puppy, she did want to please him. Perhaps she thought this was her chance, but she thought that every time he came and got her for training.

Feeling the puppy nuzzling against her calf she reaches down and scratches its muzzle. Its deep, chocolate-brown eyes gaze up at her with the pure, sweet innocence of a puppy. Dak'tari lets out a tiny giggle as the puppy's mouth drops open and its tongue droops over the side. Its tongue snakes out, covering her fingers in a thin sparkling layer of saliva, as she stands to follow the old man down the hall.

He leads her to a stairway at the end of the hall that goes both up and down. Dak'tari runs down the hall catching up with the old man as he places a foot on the stairway leading down. They continue downward two levels, the puppy plopping down the stairs is caught twice by Dak'tari, keeping it from going tail over-ears down the stairs.

At the end of the stairs, they enter a massive room. Its walls, covered in black marble, are spider-webbed with red veins, looking as if a mad man has flung blood all over the walls in the throes of his insanity.

Entering the arena-sized room from the south, Dak'tari sees suspended upon the east and west walls a cornucopia of deathinflicting devices. Every weapon known, and some unknown, to mortals covers these two walls. Four large caldrons are placed upon the area floor, each one full of glowing coals. Instead of banishing the shadows, they seem to bolster them, causing them to dance upon the walls and swallow whole sections of the room in darkness.

Leading Dak'tari and her puppy to a section of the east wall, he stops before an immense rack of daggers. Looking up Dak'tari gasps in delight as tiny beams dance upon their edges. The light reflected by the jewels in some of their hilts resembles thin rays of sunshine bursting through a storm cloud.

Squatting down next to her the old man turns her from the wall to face him. "It's time you received your first weapon." He speaks to her as if he was a college professor instructing a student, instead of an adult addressing a four-year-old child. He does not speak down to her but tells her clearly what is required of her. Here is what you need to do. Now do it. "Look at those weapons on the wall." He turns her till she is facing the wall. "Now close your eyes." Dak'tari closes her eyes. "Now child listen. Listen for the blade which is calling you." The old man's voice drops to a whisper, his breath just barely stirring the air around her ears. "Listen for *your* blade."

Dak'tari, keeping her eyes closed, opens herself up to the darkness of the void. She sees nothing. She hears nothing. She is nothing. Then from the deepest inner reaches of herself, she hears it. At first nothing more than the sound of a gentle breeze through the wispy branches of a willow tree. Dak'tari focusing on that sound coaxing it to come to her, to become stronger. Then it is there, a sweet voice dripping with honey. It's all around her, singing her name, calling her to come to it so they can be together.

Opening her eyes her gaze is instantly ensnared by the only blade she sees on the wall. It's not one of the jewel-encrusted ones, nor even one of those spectacular in design. All those have been blotted from her sight by some sort of inky blackness. Not that any of that mattered anyhow. She only wanted one blade and that one was staring her in the face. A stiletto, so black as to almost seem as if there was a hole in the wall in the shape of a stiletto, instead of an actual blade hanging there. Its twelve-inch blade was made of some sort of unknown black material, honed to a needle-sharp point. The hilt, formed from the same black substance, was wrapped in a black leather.

Dak'tari raises her right hand and points to the stiletto that is her choice. The old man easily picks her up by the waist and lifts her towards the spot where she is pointing. Holding her up, he notices the stiletto as her tiny fist closes around it. Ever so slightly a frown crosses his face as she removes the weapon from the wall. His look changes to one of extreme interest, as he sees the way Dak'tari handles the blade. Though a thin blade, the stiletto looks as if it should be too heavy for the small girl. But she holds it easily with one hand, neither struggling with point or pommel. The blade sits in her small hand as if it was created just for her.

The old man places her back on the floor, the blade twinkling in her hand. The blade does not reflect light in a normal manner, instead, it seems to capture the light and suck it into itself. The light looked like tiny black holes trapped upon its surface, winking in and out of existence along its tar-black length.

Turning, he walks to a black stone block set in the center of the room. Set on one end of the dark alter is a chalice, made from a skull dipped in gold. At the other end sits a glowing bowl of coals with a rod sticking out of its center. Dak'tari follows him, proudly holding her blade, as the puppy bounces along behind her.

When they reach the altar, the old man scoops her and the puppy up and sets them down upon the altar. He grabs Dak'tari under her chin, his yellowed fingernails digging into her cheeks. She tries to pull away, but the nails only dig deeper, causing droplets of blood to well from around his nails and roll down her cheek. When he speaks there is not a hint of kindness or gentleness in his voice. "Today you learn about trust and discipline." Removing his hand from her cheeks he plucks a hair from her head. Then he removes a gooey brown ball from a sleeve and kneads the hair into it. Gruffly he seizes the puppy by the scruff of the neck and feeds it the ball with her hair.

The change in the puppy is almost instantaneous. Saliva commences to drip from its mouth, and its hackles rise as its insane eyes focus on Dak'tari. Growling it lunges for her throat, its needlesharp teeth clamping onto her arm as she instinctively throws it in front of her face.

Dazed, her young mind not comprehending what has happened to her puppy, she is sent tumbling backward off the alter.

Slamming into the floor, sparks flash and dance in front of her eyes as her head bounces off the hard surface.

The impact jars the rabid puppy loose, tearing a jagged gash in her arm. Regaining its footing the pup whirls back around, eyes bloodshot, soft white coat bristling and matted, slavering jaws dripping blood to launch itself back at the stunned girl.

Her heart flutters like a hummingbird's wings, sending the blood pounding into her confused brain. The all-consuming sound of a ship's drum cadence, set for ramming speed, echoes within her skull. Nothing exists, not the room, not her ravaged arm, and certainly not the crazed beast that was just moments ago her only friend. Only the soothing, mind-numbing wump, wump, wump of her heartbeat can possibly be real. So she covers herself in this tranquil and relaxing reality instead of the cruel and cold one which is facing her now.

A voice thunders through the hammering veil, shattering her catatonic state. "STRIKE DAMN YOU! STRIKE NOW!"

The deep, gravelly voice commands instant obedience. The onyx stiletto vaults forward, Dak'tari's petite hand merely along for the ride, and slams into the pup behind its shoulder blades. The puppy lets out a soul-wrenching, quivering yelp as the dark stiletto impales its heart. Shuddering once it collapses upon Dak'tari's panting chest.

For the first time since hitting the ground, Dak'tari opens her eyes. Staring back at her are the frozen, glassy eyes of her canine companion. Its tongue lolling from its blood-covered muzzle, as it lays splayed across her chest. All the ferociousness gone, erased by the smoothness of death, it looks once again like the legged little cottonball that she so loved and adored.

Snatching the carcass of the pup off of Dak'tari, the old man flings it unceremoniously onto the alter. He then grabs Dak'tari by her pale white throat and lifts her up till she is at eye level with him. Staring into her vacant, hollow eyes, he gruffly strikes her with the back of his left hand. The slap echoes through the chamber of horrors to be lost within the darkness above.

Dak'tari's unearthly eyes blink once, returning her to reality. As awareness dawns on her, as to what has just happened, her bottom lip starts to quiver as tears start to form around the corners of her eyes.

THWACK! The old man strikes her another sharp blow across the face. "Tears are not allowed!"

Promptly her tears dry up as the scarlet handprints of the old man begins forming on her blanched cheek. In the place of tears comes pure, unadulterated, soul-consuming hatred. Before realizing what she is doing, her hand with the deadly blade still clutched within it races towards the old man's heart.

If not for the antediluvian hand cutting off her windpipe, Dak'tari would have yowled in anguish. Before she had a chance to blink her eyes, the jet stiletto still clutched within her hand, had found its way to the middle of her back with the old man's help. As her legs feebly kick at empty space and her eyes start to grow dim from lack of oxygen, the old man sets her down on the altar.

"Very good my child." His knife slit of a mouth turns upwards to show his yellowed teeth in a grin of pride. "Your first lesson is almost over. Just one last thing and we're through for the day. Sever your dog's head, place it in the chalice and give it to me."

She glares at the old man, the rage and hatred of all the demons and devils of hell are imbued within those four-year-old eyes. Turning she looks upon the lifeless husk before her, her eyes softening as they fall upon the deceased puppy. She starts to shake as tears start to well up when the voice, she heard as she lay upon the floor, returns to her. Gentle and soothing it comforts and surrounds her. "Steady little one now is not the time for tears. This is something you must do. Don't worry for I am with you. I will always be with you. My dear sweet love. My Dak'tari."

The pungent rusty scent of blood tickles her nose as she inhales the life essence of the slain canine. From deep within the child a switch is flicked by the soft sweet scent of the blood. A sheet of darkness slips over and covers all visages of humanity inside the half-human child. A four-year-old dies, freeing a raging hell-borne furnace of hatred and rage. Her eyes narrow to dagger-thin slits, their sharpness rivaling the edge of her vile blade, as the red flecks blazing below her lowered lids flash like supernovas in their midnight blue heaven.

A quiver of ecstasy courses through her little body, as all innocence and purity is expunged from her soul. A half-smile caresses the left corner of her mouth as she removes the head of the mongrel cur in one clean, fluid stroke. The half-smile glides across her lips, in what would be a sweet cherubic look of an angel, if not for the flames of pure nefarious hatred glaring from her eyes. Snatching the head up by the ears she places it into the chalice and hands it over to the old man.

II

Sitting on the floor of her darkened room, alone except for her loss, pain, and intense burning hatred, she wonders who or what that voice was that had come to her. Then a warm, gentle presence envelopes her, whispering seductively into her ear.

You did well my love. Very well indeed." Though spoken with love and kindness, something horrifying and evil dwells within that voice. Instantly Dak'tari falls in love with it.

Who are you?" She asks.

The voice comes again. "I am all and nothing. I am he who waits in the shadows. I am he who you will find in the tip of a blade and the hollows of a noose. I am he who laughs when babies die and cities burn. I am the darkness in a pit and the scream of the tortured. I am your mother, your father, your teacher, your lover. FOR I AM UTHANOR!"

A force then swirls around Dak'tari completely engulfing her, it swirls faster and faster. Lifting her from the floor it sweeps her up in its whirling vortex, spinning, and spinning, forever spinning. All the horrors and pains of the world assail her at once tearing her apart, putting her back together, and tearing her apart again. She tries to scream but she has no voice, no throat, no body, no way to express the horrors inflicted upon her. All she can do is ride upon the storm and allow Uthanor to have his malicious way with her. Dak'tari feels the excruciating agonies of being disemboweled, flayed, drawn and quartered, burned alive, and any other torment and torture that this god of hate can devise. He then thrusts upon her the horrors of her birth; taking the place of her mother, she relives the experience of her conception and birth. The rape, birthing, and beheading are all hers to relive and endure. As the tortures of her body subside, her head feels as if it will explode, as Uthanor crams all the knowledge he deems she will need to serve him into her head at once. Skill in arms and combat flood into her brain, as does the knowledge of torture and poisons and information concerning Tamora and its inhabitants.

Finally, the pain and horror recede from her mind, followed by all the sweet pleasures of a lover's caress and the orgasmic ecstasy of a young girl's virginity gently and lovingly taken from her.

"Now my love, you know all the pleasures and pain of the world. So you should fear no one and nothing." Uthanor's voice whispers. "I have given you all the skills and knowledge you shall need to serve me. Trust in me. Follow me. Do my bidding and love only me and you shall rule over this world as my consort. Now go my love and show the Brotherhood what it means to be my chosen."

The voice then departs, followed by the vortex that was keeping her suspended in the air. Dropping to the floor in a drained and exhausted heap lies a gorgeous, full-bodied, blonde, twenty-one yearold woman with midnight-blue eyes dotted with red flecks.

III

Dak'tari strides confidently into the main chamber with the gold throne and ebony table, naked except for her stiletto held within her right hand. Facing the old man she states flatly, "I have come in the name of he who mortals fear to name but we call Uthanor. "She then bows towards him.

"So it is time." This was not a question, just a simple statement to no one in particular.

The men gathered around the table rise in shocked amazement. Realizing that the woman before them was Dak'tari, they were just not sure how the transformation had come about. If they had been normal men, the sight of this exquisite beauty would have aroused some part of their manhood. But trained as they were to forego the pleasures of the flesh they were not distracted by her nakedness. Instead, they sensed the danger she now represented to them.

Glancing towards their master, who with a nod of his head indicates his approval, they draw their weapons and leap towards the naked figure before them.

Still facing the old man, her right arm arcs backward towards the first of her attackers, without even turning to look at them. As the short stiletto sweeps towards the rear it begins to elongate into a jet black katana, smoothly passing through the necks of two of her attackers. As the bodies hit the floor, still pumping blood from their severed stumps, she leaps into the air. Spinning she kicks one of the severed heads, sending it slamming into the stomach of another adversary, doubling him over. She then brings her katana down, adding his head to the two already on the floor.

Going into a split, she drops beneath the sword stroke of another black-clad assailant. Her dark blade sweeps around, separating his torso from his waist.

Scooping up a handful of entrails from her latest victim, she rises, spins, and plays out the intestines through her fingers making a gruesome length of rope. Flinging it out, it wraps around the throat of another member of the Brotherhood like a bullwhip. Yanking him towards her she buries her blade, which has reverted into a stiletto, into his heart.

The remaining seven members of the Brotherhood pause, taken off-guard by the savage fury and quickness of their brethren's deaths. For the five brothers were dead in less than ten seconds. All this from a woman who was but a four-year-old child just this morning. Never had one, much less five, of their number been dispatched so quickly and efficiently.

Staring at the she-demon before them, covered in blood yet not a drop of it her own, they wait and see what she will do next. She just glares back at them through those midnight blue eyes, the red flecks flashing in deadly fury.

"Are you and our lord sated yet?" The old man asks, still sitting on his gold gilded skull throne.

Dak'tari's arm shoots out like lightning. A one-eyed, black-clad assassin is pinned to the wall, through the right shoulder by a jet black javelin. Calmly walking up to him, Dak'tari thrust her hand into his chest. Grabbing his heart she rips it out, tossing it onto the floor. Squashing it with her foot she watches his life drain from his one eye, like the blood draining from the gaping hole in his chest.

"Now I' m sated," she says, pulling the javelin from the body and letting it fall to the gore-strewn floor.

Walking out the chamber, she heads for the baths, the stiletto once again in her hand.

IV

Relaxing in the baths, the hot water coming from out of hot springs located deep within the mountains core, Dak'tari washes the blood and gore from her hair and body. Feeling quite pleased and enamored with her newly acquired skills and knowledge, she smiles a wicked little smile. Running her hands slowly she caresses her body, starting at her feet and ending with her fingers sliding through her hair, exhilarated in her newfound womanhood. Quietly and lovingly she whispers, "Thank you, my lord, my love, my Uthanor."

"You did well my love." The voice of her lord embracing her again." Yes, I'm very pleased with you."

As the words come to her she feels a thrill of ecstasy, as her hand gently slides along her inner thigh.

"Of course this was nothing. I have plans for you my love, great plans indeed." As he speaks Dak'tari sits up paying close attention.

"What do you require of me? Please tell me," she begs, the pain to please her love is as tangible as her quaking voice and quivering body.

"The old man shall tell you. The first part has already been set into motion. Go back to your room and wait for him. I have left you one last gift there. Now go and listen to him well, for he has served me faithfully for millennia." And with that said the voice leaves her again.

Rising quickly from the baths, Dak'tari hurries to her room to find the old man already there sitting on her cot.

"Come little one and sit." He says, patting the spot on the bed next to him. Though now a woman, and standing a good six inches over his gnarled frame, he will always consider her his 'little one.'

She sits down next to the old man, her naked body glistening from the water droplets still clinging to her hair and body. Reflecting the eerie light from the arm sconces, the droplets blink as if they were the unholy eyes of creatures locked within the deepest pits of hell. Yet they still seem to reflect more humanity than her own dark eyes.

"Our Lord, my love, said that you would tell me what was required of me. "She says, locking those baneful eyes upon him, waiting for his reply.

"I have a few things to tell you before I inform you of what our Lord requires of you." His sickly yellow eyes in turn lock onto hers.

"Such as?" She asks indifferently, not caring, the only thing that matters to her is what her beloved requires of her. But remembering the words 'to listen to him, and the fact that he has served her beloved far longer than she can imagine, she waits semipatiently for him to say whatever he feels necessary at his own pace and time.

"Over two thousand years ago," he begins, as his eyes seem to drift off to a time long ago. "A dark force escaped the void and crept across Tamora. For long it searched for someone or something it could seduce to serve its dark will. First, it tried Orcs, Trolls, Hobgoblins, and other fearsome and loathsome creatures, but each turned out to be inadequate in one way or another."

"Then finally it came across one perfectly suited to its needs. A human poor and lonely, cast aside by even the dregs of humanity. But it had two attributes that drew the dark force to it. His quick intelligence, something the other creatures lacked, and a heart as cruel and black as the impenetrable void from which it had escaped." He pauses for a moment as the pathetic lighting in the room seems to dim and flicker.

"That was you?" Dak'tari asks, a slight reverence for the old man starting to shine within those red-flecked eyes again.

"Yes, that was I." His eyes return from the past as he rises from Dak'tari's side and crosses over to the opposite side of the room. Standing under the light he whispers, "Cantanis." The sickly light, casting shadows upon his withered head, makes it look even more skeletal than Dak'tari thought possible.

"Cantanis?" Dak'tari asks, not sure if she heard correctly.

The old man whirls, his face a mask of seething anger. His eyes narrow to slits and tear into Dak'tari. "You will never say that name again!" He hisses, then as quickly as his anger arose it dissipates.

Walking back he once again sits next to Dak'tari. Clutching Dak'tari's thigh in his claw-like grip, he whispers, "Yes, Cantanis."

As the blood starts to well up from around the claws embedded in Dak'tari's soft, pale thigh, she does not wince, pull away or otherwise show any indication of the discomfort of the claws digging into her flesh. She just sits, looking at the old man, waiting for him to continue.

"That name has not been uttered by a living soul for almost two thousand years." He continues after a moment's silence. "Not since our dark lord was banished back into the void. But back then it was mine." Relinquishing his hold on Dak'tari's leg, his eyes once again drift back into the past.

"Cantanis," he begins again, "a voice said to me. It was the most beautiful voice I had ever heard." Something only slightly akin to a smile touches his gaunt features. "Glancing around, I saw no one. A soft laughter then touched my ears. 'Where are you? Who are you?' I called out. 'I am nowhere and everywhere. I am nothing and I am everything. I am Uthanor.' The sweet woman's voice cooed to me. As she said her name I felt as if I was wrapped in a dark, foreboding, yet oh so sweet and loving, embrace."

Then Dak'tari saw something she never expected from this ancient assassin---he smiled. A real smile of joy and remembered happiness, that even lit up those cold and unforgiving eyes. This more than anything shocked her the most. She grew, even more, intent on his story.

"'Serve me, obey me, love me my dear Cantanis; and I will grant you the strength and power to destroy those that have wronged you. I shall make you my general, you shall lead my armies, conquer my enemies and rule this land as my consort.'" Dak'tari hearing this raises her eyebrows in shock.

"Yes, I know little one. That is what our dark lord promised you." He says, stroking Dak'tari's cheek with a thumb. "For now it is your turn."

Dropping his hand he inserts them both into his sleeves. With his arm crossing his chest, he seems to diminish in size. "Of course I accepted!" He continues. "Wrapped within the folds of her darkness I was invincible. She granted me all that she promised. Though I was an assassin of no small repute back then, I was nothing compared to what I became after she bestowed her gifts upon me. All the skills and power I possess, I received wrapped within her loving embrace! And in return, I gave her my body, my soul, and my eternal love!"

He rises from the cot, racing around the room in exultation and the remembered glory that was his. He flings his hands from his sleeves and shaking them towards the heavens, he yells, "VICTORY WAS OURS!"

He drops his arms and spins on Dak'tari, hate blazing in his eyes. "Ours I say. Till we were betrayed!" He spits the words out as if they were poison-tipped daggers.

Dak'tari leaps up, her body quaking with unbridled fury. "Who..." She loses her voice for a moment, choked from the overload of emotion. She swallows the bile that was rising in her throat. She continues again in almost a whisper, fighting to control her anger." Who would dare to betray my beloved?!!!" The red flecks in her eyes flash like exploding stars. Cantanis' dark heart fills with a faint twinge of pride, as he thinks to himself. *Yes, she will do very well.*

"Gauntlar, Disatara, and Lothar." Cantanis says, addressing Dak'tari, his voice filled with disgust.

"The dark gods?" Dak'tari blurts.

"Yes," He hisses, "Along with their kin, lead by Maximus." Cantanis spits on the ground as if even saying the name is poison to his lips.

"Our dark lord had recruited the three. Gauntlar for his dominion over the orcs and their kin. Disatara for her dominion over the dragons and the mages of darkness. And Lothar for his jealousy and hatred towards Maximus and the gods of light."

Cupping Dak'tari's face with both hands, he glares into her flashing eyes. "We will not make that mistake again! As a matter of fact, we, or I should say you, will avenge that betrayal!" Releasing his hold on Dak'tari's face, he resumes his pacing, as Dak'tari stands there trembling in an uncontrollable desire to unleash her fury on something or someone.

"Our dark army had the forces of light on the edge of defeat!" The old man says continuing with his tale. "Our dragons controlled the skies, having killed or sent the dragons of light off to lick their wounds. Our army had conquered all the lands, except for one last bastion of light. REATHA!" He spews the name of the hated city from his mouth as if it was a curse. His fist shoots out, slamming into the wall, shattering one of the black stone blocks with a sharp crack.

Spinning around, as the stone shards rain down upon the floor, he faces Dak'tari. The old man speaks in a whisper as if ashamed to relive the moment. "Then my dragons veered from the wall and flew off into the distance. The mages vanished, teleporting off to who knows where. Then my army. *My grand army.*" His voice rises a notch then settles back down. "That had crushed nearly all of

Tamora beneath its heels, turned on me." The last words are almost inaudible as if even now he had trouble believing it was possible.

After a moment's pause he continues, his voice strong and firm again. "At first I didn't realize what had happened. Then it hit me. It was as if something had ripped my soul from me. "His voice quiets again." She was gone."

Suddenly he reaches out and clutches Dak'tari's arm. His eyes leap out from the shadows and ensnare hers in a piercing gaze. "I flew into a rage of despair, killing I don't know how many of the treacherous beast in my red haze." He lets lose her arm as his gaze dims. "Then I found myself alone. Weeks had passed and I was far from the plains of Reatha. It was then that I started to cry, it was the only time in my life I have ever cried. Lost and confused, I started to search for what had happened to my beloved. I knew she was gone, gone back to the void where I could not reach her. But how? That was what l needed to know. For nearly two-hundred years I searched. Then I heard of an ancient witch that lived in the Meranox Swamp. Holding no allegiance to god nor man, just to the acquisition of knowledge. I questioned her, at first she denied any knowledge of what had happened to my beloved. She then saw the error of her ways and finally told me what I needed to know." A visage of a malicious smile turns up the left side of his mouth. "It took quite a while to extract all the information from her. But she did eventually tell me all she knew, in the hopes that she would at least be able to keep her head. Which of course she did not." He shrugs his shoulders in an indication of 'oh well, too bad.'

"On the day of the final battle, Gauntlar, Disatara, and Lothar had struck a deal with Maximus." Clinching his jaw he hisses between grating teeth. "And the fools accepted! Instead of all of Tamora, they settled for parts! Pelnox, Thera, Traxess, The Northern Waste and the Meranox Swamp. The fools!" He says rising from the cot in a near rant. "They made a bargain for some of the worst land in Tamora when they could have had the choicest!" Again his fist snakes forward, this time the whole room shakes as four blocks shatter, leaving a gaping hole in the wall.

"For two thousand years, I have waited for the time which has finally arrived. The day our lord would be free and ready to extract his revenge upon the heads of the betrayers!"Again he takes Dak'tari's face into his writhed hands. "The day you would be born and ready to embrace your destiny."

The last sentence sends a thrill of exultation coursing through Dak'tari. "So I will lead my beloved's army and crush his foes beneath us?" Thrusting out her chest a large smile of pride crosses her face.

"No, another has been chosen to lead the army when it is ready." Dak'tari slumps as if punched in the gut. The smile disappears from her face to be replaced by disappointment and despair. "My love does not have faith in me." It is barely a whisper.

The old man then raises her eyes to face him. "No little one, you will not lead the army." Then a malicious grin splits his face as he adds. "You shall exact revenge upon those that betrayed us! *You shall kill the gods!*»

V

"Kill the gods!" Dak'tari ejaculates, a little more than slightly shocked. "But how?"

"It is what you were bred for." The smile leaves the old man's face to be replaced by a forlorn look of disappointment. "It is something that even I can not do." He falls silent for a brief moment before continuing. "For you, little one, are not wholly born of this world."

A look of bewilderment crosses Dak'tari's eyes, but before she can say anything the old man begins speaking again. "Yes, your father is a human born of this world. But your mother... she was a demon bitch spawned in the deepest pits of hell. It's her blood that gives you the power to slay the gods."

Slowly Dak'tari plops down on the cot, overwhelmed by this revelation. Then looking up, her dark eyes, her mother's eyes, grasp the yellowed orbs of the old man's. "I always knew I was different... somehow." She says softly.

Gently taking her under the chin, his eyes try to peer into the midnight blue windows of her soulless form. "Oh yes, you are different, little one. You have never seen your reflection, have you? No, of course not." He answers before Dak'tari has a chance to reply.

Reaching into one of his bellowing sleeves he extracts a small mirror and hands it to her. The first thing, really the only thing, she notices is her eyes. The rounded-almond shape, filled with the deep blue midnight of a clear winter's night, is punctuated by the flaring red sparks that dance within their depths.

Taking the mirror back from her, he reinserts it back into its place in his sleeve. "Those are the most perceptible of the gifts your mother bestowed on you. Since the kindling of your mother's blood, by our dark lord, you will start to gain the dark gifts of demon-kind as time goes on and the need arises." Stroking her cheek he goes on. "You are the first mating of a human and demon-spawn and what that entails even I can not say. But this I do know, no weapon crafted without the assistance of magic can harm you."

Dropping his hand from her cheek he gathers her hands within his. "This also I know, and is why you were bred. A child spawned by a mortal and an immortal has the power to destroy the immortals. That is why at the beginning of creation the gods of Tamora and the denizens of hell made a pact forbidding mating with mortals. For none of them wished that a child of their own making would come back to slay them."

"Then why did my mother consent?"

The old man releases Dak'tari and leans back into a shadow eclipsing a corner of the cot, and begins to chuckle. His laugh is full of evil and malicious pleasure. "She did not. She was tricked by our dark lord, raped by your father, and killed at the moment of your birth to conceal the secret." Peering from the shadows his eyes narrow as he watches for Dak'tari' s reaction. "Does this bother you?"

Dak'tari ponders this for a moment, realizing this was a part of the experience that her beloved had thrust upon her in their "mating". She mulls over the information she has been given so far. Though appearing as an adult, full of intelligence and knowledge, she was still in reality just a young girl, a child of four. Full of the naivete and ignorance of a child, her mind tends to focus on only one thought. The complete and utter desire to please and not disappoint her beloved. Just as any child believes that a beloved parent can do no wrong, so she feels towards Uthanor. So after a moment's hesitation, while she realizes that the only thing important to her is the desire to make Uthanor proud.

"Bother me? No, it does not bother me. She served her purpose. Besides her sacrifice allows me to serve my beloved."

Smiling, the old man's skeletal face reappears from out of the gloom. "Very good little one." He says with a touch of grandfatherly pride. "She had to be killed and you ripped from her stomach. For if you would have been birthed, it would have alerted the immortals to your existence. And we could not allow that. At least not until we are ready."

"And that time is now!" She says, standing up, squaring her shoulders, and tossing her hair. As she does tiny droplets, which were still clinging to her hair, fly across the room like little meteors as the light bounces from them.

"Patience!" He hisses, as a hand clasps Dak'tari's face in a vicelike grip. "Our Lord and I have waited for two-thousand years! You can learn to wait a while! We will not lose again because a child chooses to run headlong into situations she can not possibly grasp! Do you think you will be able to just summon the gods and stab them one by one?!" The yellowed talons, on the end of his fingers, tear into her cheeks. "Do you understand?"

"Y-Y-Yes." She stammers, shocked by his vehemence.

"No, you don't!" He says, dropping his hand. "But you will."

Clasping his hands behind his back, he once again starts to pace the small black room. "Tomorrow before first light you shall leave here and go to Passail, in the land of Traxess on the shores of Draxess Lake. There you will find the High Temple of Gauntlet. His high priest Tha'gal possesses the Fingerbone of Gauntlet. With this relic, and the assistance of some who will be 'persuaded' to help," at this, a vile grin touches his face. "We will be able to send you to the plane of Gauntlar." He spins towards Dak'tari." Whom you will then destroy! From there you will be able to traverse the planes to the other realms of the gods. And destroy each in tum!"

He stops and points to the space beneath her cot. "Look under there." He waits for Dak'tari to do as instructed.

Reaching into the blackness her hand falls upon a soft leathery object. Removing it, she sees that it appears to be a full-body suit. Completely black, with even darker, pulsating runes running along the sleeves, around the collar, and down the sides to the bottom of the legs.

As Dak'tari searches the suit looking for the clasps or ties which will allow her to put it on, the old man says. "Put your legs in there." Pointing at the neck hole.

As she does the neck hole elongates to accommodate her legs, hips, waist, bust, arms and shoulders. Finally, it closes around her neck forming around her body as if it was her skin.

"This was made," says the old man, waving a hand up and down Dak'tari's body. "From the flayed skins of dark elves. It will do three things. First, it will cloak you from anybody searching for you through magical means. Second, it will allow you to take the shape of just about any humanoid creature within three times your size. You can't become a giant or a sprite, but you can become an ogre or a gnome. Try it." He says nodding towards her. "Just picture an image in your mind and you will transform into that creature."

Dak'tari closes her eyes and furrows her brow. "No!" Exclaims the old man. "Don't strain, just picture it."

Dak'tari sees a dwarf, a creature she had seen in a picture book, with a long gray beard in her mind's eye. "Good," says the old man.

Dak'tari opens her eyes and looks down, gasping as she sees a long gray beard that nearly touches the floor. With even more surprise she notices that her legs and chest are covered in plate mail. As she reaches out to rub her hand along the armors surface, she sees five fat stubby fingers, her surprise showing through the dark brown eyes of the dwarf.

With a laugh, he replies to the query in his/her eyes. "Yes little one, the skin also changes to suit the attire of your desired subject."

Then the dwarf is gone to be replaced by a female elf, another creature from the book, in flowing robes and shining purple eyes. Then the elf is gone, followed quickly by an orc, a troll, a gnome, a goblin, and then Cantanis is staring at his features.

"Enough!" He yells, anger flaring within his eyes. Instantly he is upon her, backhanding her before she has time to realize that she has been slapped. "This is not a toy to be trifled with!"

Immediately the blonde half-demoness stands before him, with dark eyes glaring.

"Remember why you are here! Why you were created!" His yellow eyes flashed as fiercely as hers. Eventually the fires dim. "As I said before there are three properties to the suit you wear. The third is the ability for the suit to grasp onto things of its own accord freeing up your hands to do other things. The tentacles do not extend far, three to four feet at the most, but it will allow you to hold onto a wall or person, leaving your hands free to fight."

"Now get some rest, you shall be summoned in the morning. I still have much to see to." He turns and walks out the door, closing it behind him.

Dak'tari throws herself onto the small cot and stares at the ceiling. As the adrenaline courses through her body, she knows she will never fall asleep. Dreaming of tomorrow and what it shall bring, her breathing deepens, her eyelids grow heavy and she falls asleep.

VI

Dak'tari awakens as soon as the soft footsteps stop in front of her door, disappointed that her beloved had not come to her in the night. She is on her feet, wide awake with her stiletto in her hand before the door opens.

"It is time," is all the black-clad figure says before turning around and walking back down the hall to the main chamber.

Following him to the main chamber, Dak'tari finds the old man sitting on his skull-clad throne with the remainder of the Brotherhood standing before him.

"Come here." The old man orders, waving a beckoning hand towards Dak'tari. "You all know what your missions are. You will leave here and sail to the shores of Traxess. From there you will each make your way to your final destinations." Eyeing them all coldly he adds, "Do not fail!"

Dak'tari and her seven companions set sail before first light. Making their way through the fog bank and reef which guards their island, they enter the open ocean. The one sail ship, though small, is very sturdy; riding the swelling waves with ease and grace. No one speaks or makes a sound during the trip, allowing Dak'tari to stand on the bow in peace watching her first sunrise break over the horizon. She thrills at the new sensations of the sea air rushing through her hair and the tangy taste of the saltwater splashing upon her face. Free at last her heart screams, free from the confines of the oppressive Black Fortress. Free at last to clasp the reins of her destiny and serve her beloved. Free at last to stride upon Tamora as the avenging dark angel of Uthanor, and bring retribution and fear upon those who betrayed her dark lord so long ago.

Throughout the day the boat skims along the surface, with only a few gulls circling in the clear blue sky and a pair of dolphins trailing the boat to break up the scenery. Not once does Dak'tari move from her place at the prow, remaining as stiff and immobile as the wooden statues set as guards on the front of the great ships of Canthor.

Two hours after nightfall the shore comes into view, an even darker shape on an already dark horizon. The sand of the beach scrapes along the bottom bringing the boat to a stop. No sooner has it halted than Dak'tari leaps from the bow and wades the short distance ashore, while the rest of the crew drag it off the sand and return it to the ocean. As she enters the woods, that drape the shoreline, she turns to see the ship heading back down the coastline, vanish into the darkness and continue its journey to its next destination. She then enters the thick woods, which quickly close behind her, blocking her view of the water, and begins to make her way to Passail.

Chapter II

INTRODUCTIONS AND ASSASSINATIONS

I

Serpentine tendrils of ghostly white mist weave themselves along the forest floor, covering it in an unholy death shroud. Deramar, sitting in the still darkness of the night, his back resting against the trunk of a large oak tree, watches the haunting mist flow towards him. The ghastly spectral fingers caress his body, engulfing him in a blanket of muffed stillness, as they continue their journey through the forest.

Straining their way through the fog, from the southeast comes the muffled clash of steel on steel. Gathering his blanket, the total of all his possessions besides a small pouch hanging from his neck, he heads off through the forest towards the sound of combat. Dressed in a dark gray tunic and brown pants, the mist-enshrouded darkness absorbs him into itself, obliterating his presence from the world.

Making less noise than the fog itself, he glides towards the orange glowing firelight swallowed within the mist. The area around the firelight was like a gladiatorial arena from hell, filled with the dark, flittering shadows of men cursing and moaning in anguish. Stopping about ten feet from the edge of the glowing area Deramar circles around trying to determine who is killing whom.

At the glowing heart of the battle, six men surround an elegantly carved wooden wagon. The firelight plays hauntingly upon the guardian glistening plate armor. At their feet, bubbling their last breath into the moldy, leaf-covered forest floor, lay six more guards with arrows protruding from them.

"Randus!" One of the men barks, raising a shield as an arrow sinks into its face. "Take the princess and get her the hell out of here!" He punctuates his command with a meaty thump as his sword cleaves through the shoulder and breastbone of a charging attacker, covering him in the spraying blood.

"Captain Dyrgen, Lieutenant Randus is dead!" A voice replies quivering on the verge of panic.

"Son, you better keep your shit together or I will run you through myself! You hear me!" Flames of anger touching upon the commander's voice. "That goes for all of you! You all swore to give your lives defending the royal family and now is the time to prove the worth of your honor! Now damn you, boys! FIGHT! Fight till their blood or ours stains the forest floor!"

With as much sound as a shadow, Deramar silently crosses the forest floor to the base of a large oak where a black-clad assassin sits perched within its branches. Gliding up the tree Deramar creeps up behind the figure as he raises his bow to let loose another arrow into the midst of the defending knights.

As the string twangs, with the release of the arrow, Derarnar grabs the assassin's head from behind and breaks the archer's neck with a quick twist. Reaching out he grabs the bow from the lifeless fingers before it has a chance to slip to the ground and warn the other assassins of Deramar's presence.

Placing the corpse against the trunk, Deramar removes the quiver of arrows and crosses back out to the end of the branch. Scanning the trees, circling the campsite, he spies five archers in the surrounding trees and eight swordsmen on the forest floor engaging the hard-pressed, battling knights. Sighting in on his first target Deramar lets fly an arrow towards the archer in the nearest tree to the left of him. Piercing him through the eye, the deadly projectile sends him tumbling off the branch. Before the body hits the ground Deramar turns and releases another arrow into the throat of the assassin sitting in the tree to the right of him.

As the bodies hit the damp forest floor, Deramar drops from his tree, slips back into the darkness, and circles around the camp to deal with the remaining archers from within the seclusion of the night.

As Deramar dispatches the remaining assassins in the trees, Captain Dyrgen tries to pry his sword from the split skull which is hanging on to it. Letting go of his sword he turns slamming the edge of his shield up under the chin of an onrushing attacker, nearly severing the head completely from his neck. "May the shriveled up old womb that bore you feel that!" Reaching down he grabs his sword, kicking the head that was sticking to it off. Turning he prepares to face the next attacker which is rushing towards him. Before reaching him though the attacker arches his back, drops his sword, and collapses at Drygen's feet with an arrow protruding from his back. In quick succession the rest of the attackers are dispatched by arrows from Deramar or hacked down by the remaining blood-covered knights.

A half-dressed knight, welding a horseman's pick as if he was driving circus tent pegs home, deals with the final assailant, slamming it into the top of the last assassin's skull with enough force to pop the eyeballs from their sockets, sending them flying out to bounce off his tunic covered chest.

As he steps on the eyeless, crushed skull to pry his pick from the corpse, Deramar enters into the firelight. He holds the bow down by his side with one hand as he raises his other in a show of non-hostility. When the battered knights catch sight of him, he throws down the bow and raises that hand outward.

"I'm not here to fight. At least not with you."

Deramar says smiling, nodding towards the body lying at Dyrgen feet. The arrow still stuck in his back points towards the fog-shrouded heavens like a finger of death.

"So I guess this is your handy work?" Dyrgen says, kicking the body. "And the ones in the trees as well?" Deramar just nods.

The captain of the knights slowly looks Deramar up and down with the critical eye of a veteran soldier." Well, I can't say I'm not grateful." He finally states, removing his blue and white plumed helm, he reveals a bald head and a thick, fiery red beard and braided mustache, extending a full ten inches past his upper lip, where the ends are kept secured with two sparkling gold bound rubies. A scar starting an inch below his left eye runs down his cheek to be lost within his beard, leaving in it a streak of gray.

"Shit!" He exclaims, spitting on the body before him. "This godsdamn fog rolled up from out of nowhere with these bastards hot on its heels. I doubt if it was just good timing, that's for damn sure."

Looking over his men he shakes his head. "Rait, see if any of our men are still alive. Temar, go see to the horses. Darl, you go see if you can find out who this scum is."

After issuing his orders to all that is left of his contingent of men, he turns to the ornately carved carriage. One eye constantly stays on Deramar as he opens the door. "Are you alright your highness?" He asks someone hidden in the darkness of the carriage.

"Oh yes, Captain Dyrgen." The voice of a young girl replies. "I'm never scared when daddy lets you guard me."

"Well, your highness it makes me proud to hear you say that." He says with a bow of his head." Besides," he whispers into his beard. "I was plenty scared for the both of us."

"So can I come out now?" The girl asks.

"Not right this moment. As soon as we clear up out here we will moving out. Fog or no fog we're in no condition to stay here. The sooner we get to Stalora the happier I'll be."

Turning back towards Deramar, he adds. "If your father doesn't have my head."

"Sir," Rait says addressing the captain of the royal guard, "all the men that took wounds are dead. It appears that they used some sort of poison on their weapons."

Captain Dyrgen's face contorts into a mask of rage; slowly he breathes, fighting the desire to snatch up one of the dead assassins and rip it limb from limb. Speaking with barely contained restraint he addresses Rait, "Commence to make a pyre, we can't bring them to the elven capital with us."

"And their dead?"

"Leave them for the bloody wolves and buzzards!" His voice straining as he tries not the vent his anger on his own man.

As Rait turns to leave, Temar returns through the already thinning fog, "Well, I'll say this." He says leading four horses into the firelight. "The horses stood true to their training. All twelve were standing not twenty-five yards off in a group. The others are following right behind. How many men did we lose?"

"Eight."

"Eight! But surely..."

"Poison. Now leave the horses and help Rait with the bodies."

Captain Dyrgen stands silent for a moment, running his fingers down his braided mustache before focusing his full attention back on Deramar. "Now sir, who might you be?" The anger is wiped from his voice to be replaced with the formal tone of a military officer. "And how did you stumble upon this?" He adds waving a hand across the body-littered clearing.

"My name is Deramar, Deramar Seranesta. And as for how I came to stumble upon you. I was camped not far from here when I heard the sound of fighting. I saw that you were guarding a royal carriage and realized fairly quickly that you could use a little help." The last sentence is punctuated with a look at the two guards working on the funeral pyre.

Dyrgen's tone eases slightly "Well, there is no denying that you saved our asses and our ward, and for that, I must thank you. Where are you heading? You look as if you had a pretty rough time of it lately." Indicating the torn and ragged clothes.

"Nowhere in particular. I've just been kind of wandering since I left Pasadera. You are the first humans I've seen in over a month."

"Pasadera, huh. I guess since you're not still there you fought with Prince Andrus?"

"Till our defeat at Terdaron Crossing," Deramar states through a clenched jaw.

Darl walks back from the night-enshrouded forest into the glowing firelight looking like a soldier of hell. His long black hair, matted with drying pieces of gore, flares from his head like the mane of a rabid lion. Orange flames, from the fire, dance within his narrowed, ferrous eyes reflecting the burning, unfulfilled fury burning within his soul. He clinches his white-knuckled fingers around the haft of his dripping pick as if to channel his fury into his weapon to be unleashed upon the next poor fool that dares cross him.

Splashed in the blood of his foes, his once white tunic is near black from the drying blood. Two circular splotches, blazing slightly darker, resemble two little suns equally spaced on either side of his breastbone, as if they were dyed there, marking the impact of his last opponent's eyes.

Stopping beside the two men he addresses his captain. "Six in the trees, killed by him." He nods towards Deramar and even though he speaks steadily, the burning blood lust rides upon the undercurrents of the tone. "And twelve in the clearing. There are no survivors and no identifying marks or items. Other than their clothes and weapons they carried nothing. Their weapons seem to be covered in some sort of substance. Poison," he spits out the word. "I presume."

"Collect their weapons, except for one, and throw them on the pyre. They will make a decent offering for our men, and bring the one back to me. We'll see if the elven mages can determine something from it." The captain says rolling his head, cracking the vertebrae in his neck, somewhat helping to relieve his tension.

He then turns back to Deramar, "We're heading to the elven capital Stalora. You're welcome to ride with us there if you want. We have a horse you can use till we get there. What the hell, I guess you can just have the beast as a small show of gratitude. We have extra, now," he adds bitterly. "And I' m sure the king would like to thank you personally for the aid in saving his daughter."

Turning he walks to where Rait and Temar, done stacking the wood, have begun laying the fallen knights on top of the pile for the conflagration. After the bodies have been laid atop the pyre, they begin to lay the enemy weapons upon their still chests; with the exception of a bow, quiver of arrows, two long swords, and two dirks, the bow, arrows, one of the swords and dirks, with the poison wiped clean are kept by Delamar. The other dirk, with the poison still intact, is wrapped in a piece of cloth and handed over to Dyrgen to be given to the elven mages. Taking the item he places it into a compartment beneath the carriage.

Turning from the carriage, he walks to the fire and removes a flaming branch. As the men gather around the altar of self-sacrifice the door to the carriage opens, allowing a small demure figure to be released from its velvety confines.

Ignoring her bodyguard's advice, Princess Lorreianna heads towards the pyre with a small bouquet of wildflowers, which she had picked earlier in the day, clutched within her small hands. Scattering them on top of the fallen knights, with tears streaking down her face, she whispers slowly. "I'm sorry, may the gods be kinder to you in the next life than they were in this one." She then turns, wiping the tears away with the sleeve of her sky-blue dress, and goes to stand next to Captain Dyrgen.

Placing a huge hand on her tiny shoulder, he looks down at her.

"You have nothing to be sorry for princess. They died in battle and they died with honor."

"Yet still, they died protecting me." The tears slowly dripped down her cheeks.

"It was their job and it was what they were trained for." Patting her shoulder, he leaves her side and walks up to the mound, and thrusts the fiery brand into the waiting tinder placed under the bodies. "May you guard the hall of Maximus as well as you guarded the royal family."

"Detail!" The captain bellows, bringing the surviving knights snapping to attention.

"Salute!" As one of their right hands, clutched in a fist, thump against their chest.

"Ready, two!" As the men drop their salute Dyrgen turns to them.

"Alright my surviving wolves let's get the hell out of here and to the safety of Stalora. Princess if you please." He adds lifting an arm towards the carriage.

Addressing Deramar, once again, who has been standing by silently and patiently by the horses. "Well, have you decided to join us and sample a king's gratitude? Or do you wish to stay out here and wander the woods some more?"

"As exciting as staying out here sounds, I wouldn't mind sampling civilization again. So with that being said, I would be honored to join you."

"Good, good." The captain says slapping Deramar on the back. "Then let's be off. Rait, Temar you take the carriage. Darl, you take rear guard. I and our newfound friend here will take a point, so we can get acquainted. Now, damn it men stay on your toes, we're not out of the woods yet." Looking around he shakes his head at his own unintentional pun. The men move to their horses, take their positions, and begin moving out down the road through the darkness, with the remaining horses trailing behind them.

As the first rays of the sun kisses the dew-covered grass of a meadow, causing it to glisten as if it was strewn with tiny fragments of quartz, the greatly reduced company exits the dark confines of the forest.

Dyrgen, relaxing slightly now that his field of vision has opened up, turns to Deramar. "Now that we're out of there. How did you come to find yourself in this place?"

"It's a long story," Deramar replies softly.

"Well, we have six hours before we reach the elven capital, and not much to do till we get there. Besides I can't very well present you to King Talric without having some kind of background information on you."

"Fair enough," Deramar says, raising his head to stare out in front of him, his eyes going blank in pained remembrance. Quietly, almost in a whisper, he begins his tale.

"I had a small farm in the central lowlands of Pasadera, it wasn't much but it kept me and my family fed. Then on a drizzly morning, as my son and I were working in the fields, the civil war between Prince Andrus and his brother Prince Fairinan came to my home." Stopping, he removes a water skin hanging from the saddle horn. Taking a sip his eyes blink once, then fades off into the distance past again.

"A year into the war Prince Fairinan made his forward thrust into the central lowlands. A forward scouting party came upon my farm. They said I was a rebel sympathizer, that I had helped them and given them food. I tried to tell them that I was just a simple farmer, that I would be happy to share my food with them also if they were hungry."

"Then their leader, a Captain Hath Kurn, may all the demons of hell toy with his soul, got off his horse and started heading towards my wife, who had come out the house, carrying our baby girl Marissa, to see what was going on. Laughing, he said, 'Oh yes, you will share.'"

"Running towards him, I demanded to know what he thought he was doing. Spinning, he whirled around catching me in the jaw with a mail-covered fist. Coming to stand over me with a spear in his hand, he leered down. 'If you must know. I plan on taking your animals and burning your farm. Then as your children watch we are all going to have our way with your wife. Afterward, we're going to slit your children's throats as your wife watches, then we will slit her throat. But don't you worry, you will be here for the whole thing.' He then took the spear and shoved it through my abdomen pinning me to the ground."

Dyrgen nods towards Deramar's side. "So that's where you picked that up?" Indicating the scar that showed through the hole in Deramar's shirt.

Looking at Dyrgen blankly he doesn't at first understand the question. Finally, he grasps what was asked of him. "Yes." He replies dropping a hand over the old wound. Realizing he still held the water skin within his white-knuckled hand, he ties it back onto the saddle horn allowing the blood to flow back into his fingers.

"I'm sorry, please go on," says the burly knight, abashed at interrupting Deramar's narrative lowers his eyes, shaking his head.

"I struggled for as long as I could." Deramar continues. "The tormented screams of my family tore vainly at my ears, just as I tore vainly at the shaft sticking up out of my body. Till finally from pain and loss of blood I lost consciousness."

"I came to, to find a group of Prince Andrus' men had come by and spotted the smoke. They were able to get me to a healer before I died from blood loss but too late to do anything for my family but give them a decent burial."

"For three years I rode and fought with the band that found me, until the defeat and capture of Prince Andrus at Tredaron's Crossing. After the execution of Prince Andrus, at the hands of his brother, I and the rest of us that were captured were led off in chains to be sold for slaves."

"One of the many skills I picked up in the war was the ability to manipulate locks and such. So one night when the guards were more lax than usual I escaped and headed into the woods. For the last three months, I've just wandered from one place to another. Then I heard the sound of fighting coming from your camp."

The creaking of the carriage wheels, the clomping of the horses' hooves, and the singing of the birds, greeting the morning sun, were the only sounds to punctuate the oppressive silence. The two men rode quietly for a few minutes, one dressed in gleaming armor, the other dressed in rags.

Dyrgen running a hand over his long mustache finally breaks the silence. "Yeah... I heard there was some ugly fighting going on over there. It's always the civilians, caught in the middle, that get the worst of it."

Nodding his head back towards the carriage Deramar asks, "Do you mind if I ask you a question?"

"What in all the hells are we doing out here, huh?" Dyrgen says shaking his head.

"That's pretty much it. It's obvious you're escorting a member of the Reatha Royal family." Again he nods back towards the carriage with the royal seal of Reatha emblazoned upon its side. A golden dragon, its wings draped protectively around a silver, flaming sword pointing towards the heavens. "And seeing as how she is too young to be Queen Talissa, I presume it must be Princess Lorreianna." He pauses looking at the captain of the royal guards; Drygen nods his fierybearded head once.

"Now the way I see it. If you were going to Stalora from Reatha you would be on the Rea-lora Commerce Way." Looking at the dirt road below them, and then glancing around waving an arm at the forest, which they had once again entered, he states. "This is not the Rea-lora Commerce Way."

"No," Dyrgen says, spitting on the dirt road. "This for damn sure is not the Rea-lora,"

Starting at the capital of Reatha, a city named after the country itself, the Rea-lora is a thirty-foot wide swath of gray granite which runs five hundred miles, along the western bank of the Heartland River and around Middle Lake, to Stalora, the capital of the elves, which is also named for their country. The massive construction is the combined work of humans, elves, and dwarves. Built two hundred years ago, after the Flame Wars, to promote freer trade and goodwill between the three races. It has garrisons posted every ten miles to ensure that traffic flows smoothly and to discourage brigands. The most prosperous area on the whole of Tamora, cities, villages, inns, taverns, and countless shops are dotted along its entire length.

Leaving the Heartland River it runs another one hundred miles, cutting through the northern part of Meradon, bypassing the Meranox Swamp. It then crosses the Sta-nessa river and enters the eastern portion of Stalora. Here stands the Mera-lora Bridge, the crowning jewel of men, elves, and dwarves. Like a divine jewel, this monument and inspiration to the creation of mortals, slopes gently up from the southeastern bank into the loving arms of life awaiting it on the northwestern bank. Spanning three hundred yards across the Stanessa river, the Mera-lora Bridge is formed on its southeastern span from white crystalline marble. Sunlight refracted by the crystalline veins, woven within the pure white marble, sparkles along the southern half like droplets of morning dew. Reaching towards the heavens, shining like golden lighthouses, are six towers tapering to a spiraling, blinding tip. Carved to resemble massive, golden unicorn horns thrust into the riverbed, they support the sweeping scrolled cables, made from the same white crystalline marble, that makes up the finishing touches to the bejeweled half of the suspension bridge.

At mid-point, the bridge changes over to elven design. Having a great affinity for nature, the elves with their magic and patience shape their surroundings from the natural world.

Two colossal, flowering vines reach out from the north-western bank to make up the framework for the northwestern half of the bridge. Grown into the likeness of its southeastern counterpart, its twisting tendrils branch off to make the towers, piles, and cables. The roadway, covered in a lush, green loam, is a five-foot-deep web of tiny interwoven strands cast from the main supports, making it just as strong and sturdy as the marble side. Performing a ballet to nature, birds, butterflies, sprites, and pixies all flutter throughout the myriad spectrum of blooms and blossoms hugging the enchanted vines. Intertwined around each other, in a lover's embrace, the two largest golden and natural towers symbolize the unity and friendship of the three nations.

After crossing the Mera-lora Bridge, the Rea-lora Commerce Way remains the lush green loam of the elves, its magical properties making it impervious to ruts and holes, till reaching the fork of the Xaxtor Waterway and the Stalora River. Branching, the road runs along both waterways, one to the elven capital which remains the lush emerald green loam. And the other to the dwarven stronghold of Xaxtor, which reverts back to the gray granite blocks.

"We're riding up from Peltas. The princess was visiting her grandmother Queen Ansyia of Meradon." His eyes constantly scanning the trees to either side of him as he continues. "King Talric has been in Stalora, talking to Principal Citizen Kash Steelstone of Xaxtor and Eminence Jerilith of the elves, hashing out some new trade agreement. He's returning home in three days and wishes his daughter to return home with him." He looks over his shoulder, back at the carriage, making sure everything was alright. "Everything's been fairly peaceful across Tamora as of late. Except for Pasadera." He adds glancing at Deramar. "Even on these backroads," again he scans the thickening woods around them, "brigand attacks have been far and few between. Those back there however were not common highwaymen."

Suddenly Dyrgen reins his horse in and thrust a fist into the air. Instantly the small column comes to a halt, weapons drawn and ready.

Clad in a material that seems to absorb the colors of the forest around him, an elf steps into the road blocking their path as if a part of the tree in front of them has come to life and left the confines of the trunk.

"Captain Dyrgen, I'm second prime Elstar. We were sent to escort you the rest of the way to Stalora." He says, in a sing-song voice, as other elves begin to appear from the trees and bushes lining the road.

"Well then Elstar, lead the way. I' II feel a lot better once we reach Stalora."

Scanning the battered caravan Elstar comments, "It appears your trip was not uneventful."

"Yea, you could say that. We were jumped by a band of cutthroats. Not sure who the hell they were, but we got some of their equipment in the hopes that your people may be able to shed a little light on that. Now if you please, can we get out of this gods-forsaken forest."

Elstar scowls, for to the elves the forest is life and a gift from the gods. It is humans who taint it. "Follow us, we shall be there within an hour." Turning he starts down the road.

"I don't think you made him very happy by insulting his forest. You know how sensitive they are about their woodlands." Deramar whispers to the red-bearded captain.

"Bugger him and his forest! I'm a soldier, not a diplomat. My job is to make sure nothing happens to my charge, not to make friends." He exclaims heading after the elf, followed by the carriage and his remaining men.

II

"By Xax's fiery beard, I's is sick of this crap!" Outraged, Principal Citizen Kash Steelstone slams a mail-encased fist down upon the intricately carved elven table. Cracking the table and overturning the decanter filled with the exquisite elven red wine, which flows across the map of Tamora like blood.

"So do you feel better?" Asks Eminence Jerilith, waving a hand at the mess the dwarven leader just made.

"Better! Better?!" The vein in the dwarf's temple throbs, as he ejects each word as if it were a curse. "What would make me feel better is if youse would pull the clay out of youse pointed ears and listen to what the hell I's am saying!" The robust dwarf quivers in anger as he glares up at the delicate elf. The thought of snapping the thin, pale neck of Jerilith crosses his mind, but war with the elves is not what he is here for. Though he would enjoy the war a hell of a lot more than this alliance he has come seeking.

Quickly King Talric decides he best step in and calm matters down. Soothingly he lays a hand on the shoulders of both leaders. "Please, what is this going to accomplish? Let's all calm down and Kash, please explain to us again what is happening in Xaxtor."

"Bring us some more wine, and ale for the Principal Citizen. And have someone clean this mess up, please. We shall move to the other room." Glancing over at a servant, standing in a corner trying very hard to be invisible, the human king indicates the doorway across the chamber.

As the three enter the chamber, it appears more of a giant covered balcony than an actual room. The balcony extends six hundred feet above the carpeted, forest floor. The branches making up the floor and balustrade are interwoven by centuries of gentle guidance and magic and then covered with a plush, emerald green moss. Thin flowering vines make up the covering for the balcony, filling the area with the sweet, euphoric aroma of life. Which of course causes Kash to start sneezing profusely.

"Damn, I's will be happy when I's get back to my's mines." He coughs, before blowing a snot rocket onto the carpeted flooring. Which causes Jerilith to cringe and screw his face up in disgust.

Jerilith shaking his head walks to the railing to gaze upon the city he so dearly loves. Talric coming up beside him lays one hand on the railing while setting his other on Jerilith's shoulder. "It is quite a beautiful sight." He states with a touch of awe. He's been to Stalora twice, but the sight of the city never fails to impress him.

Located on the fringes of the Draken Forest, Stalora sits draped in the soothing shade of the massive Leonessa Trees. Named for the goddess of nature, the Leonessa Tree trunks, some over two-hundred feet in diameter, can grow to a towering height of one thousand feet. The sweeping umbrella of branches is covered with glassy, translucent, blue-green leaves, which allows the life-giving sun access to the forest floor.

The dwellings of the elves look like all the blossoms of the world braided into glistening strands of deep green hair. Small blonde vines are nurtured and grown into the shape of the occupants' favorite flower, between large, velvety-green, moss-covered vines, which drop from the canopy above to the earth below. After the framework is created it is then covered, inside and out, with soft green moss. Finally, bestowing the breath of life upon the dwelling, they are then covered with the flowering plants they are formed to represent. Roses of all colors dance in the air, as well as lilies, tulips, posies, and daisies. There are even orange, peach, and lemon blossoms, with tiny, miniature fruits trees growing upon the delicately sculpted petals.

Running throughout the swaying city is a vast network of wide suspended walkways connecting the gargantuan trees, with smaller ones branching off, leading to the elven homes.

Having cleared his sinus and downed a pint of ale, brought to him by the servant Kash asks, "Are youse ready to listen, or do youse wish to jump? Personally I's kind of like the jump idea me's self."

"Yes, please continue," Talric says, turning from the expanse. Followed by Jerilith they sit at a table, brought in by the servants, covered with the wine-stained map.

"Now, if youse is done with the orc-shit pleasantries," Kash says, glaring at the two.

Jerilith, jaw clenched in aggravation, just nods, having just about had his fill of the gruff dwarf. While Talric, getting tired of playing the diplomat, downs a goblet of wine. Realizing though that something is obviously eating at the dwarf, who is always blunt is rarely so rude. "Now please explain what has you so troubled that you would leave your mountain home and call for this meeting?"

Exhaling, the anger visibly draining from him, the dwarf takes a seat. "Forgive my 's rudeness," he asks looking at Jerilith. "My's anger is not with youse." Jerilith nods, the tension draining from his face as he also realizes that something must seriously be wrong since dwarfs rarely apologize for anything. "But with why I'm asked youse to meet with me's. Something is wrong in the Northern Waste."

"What do you mean?" Jerilith asks, leaning over the map to view the area marked Northern Waste. Now he was truly intrigued, as was Talric, for it was quite unlike Kash, or any dwarf for that matter, to involve any of the other races in their problems, being an extremely proud folk.

"About two months ago," starts the dwarven ruler. "I's sent a patrol of thirty warriors on patrol into the Wastelands, just routine nothing special, more of an exploration than anything else. Well, after three weeks wees' had received no word or sign of thems'. Figuring maybe theys' got caught in an avalanche or something, I's sent out another thirty to search for thems'. With the instruction theys' were to report back in two weeks. Theys' never returned."

The anger starting to rise again, Kash turns to spit on the floor. Spotting the glare coming from Jerilith, he swallows his bile and continues.

"Finally having had enough I ' s sent out seventy-five hand-picked guards of the Golden Vein, as youse know theys' are mys' elite force. Two weeks later, just one returned. "His hand grasps the table threatening to splinter this one also." Before hes' died all hes' said was 'dark force.' What this force was that hes' was talking about wes' was unable to determine. The strangest thing was that hes' did not appear to die from any wounds, for hes' was unbloody. Hes' appeared to die from fright, magic, or something else. For hes' was Young when Is' sent hims' out, only sixty, but when hes' returned hes' appeared to be two-hundred or so." Slowly Kash releases his hold on the table and sits back. "Is' have since banned any farther excursions into the Wastelands, but have tripled all the guards till it can be determined what is going on up there." Draining another mug of ale, the foam clinging to his thick, proud mustache, he falls silent.

Running his finger through his thick, black beard, the king of Reatha finally breaks the silence. "What is it you propose?"

"What many can't do, perhaps a few can. What Is' suggests is a small force comprised of the three races to journey in the Wastelands and see if theys' can find out what is going on, for this threat I's fear concerns usis' all. Then return back and inform us what this 'dark force' is, so wees' can then plan ours' next course of action."

Jerilith, rising from his seat, returns to the balcony. Gazing upon his city, he sighs. Catching sight of something, he peers more closely, then a smile crosses his angular features. Turning back to Kash, "I agree to your proposal, but we shall have to work out the details tomorrow for something has just rode up. Talric, I believe your daughter has just arrived."

Moving quickly to stand next to Jerilith, Talric's face breaks out into a huge grin. Walking up, the dwarven leader places a hand on the human's arm. Looking at the dwarf, the human says "You have my support also, but if you will excuse me there is someone I need to go see."

Kash's hand closes upon the human's shoulder, in an unusual show of affection for a dwarf. "Go, go see yours' daughter, be happy with hers' now. For Is' fear, the happy times are coming to an end."

III

Washed, fed, and dressed in a new attire provided by the elves, Deramar relaxes on a couch waiting to be presented to the king of Reatha. The couch made from soft green moss with rose petals interwoven into it emits a delicate and relaxing aroma that soothes the soul and banishes all tension.

Having entered Stalora, Captain Dyrgen and the carriage with Princess Lorreianna were taken to the main entrance of the 'Grace of Leonessa'. By far the largest tree in the city, it was easily three hundred feet in diameter and towered nearly seventeen hundred feet high, housing the royal family and the seat of government for Stalora. While Deramar and the rest of the knights were taken to a smaller entrance, on the far side of the massive tree. Waiting for them were a flock of young elven maidens to take care of them and show them to their rooms.

Deramar is instantly awake, having fallen asleep on the plush, intoxicating couch, as a soft tapping comes from the door to his room.

"Come in." He says, rising from the couch.

The door opens, allowing an elderly, gray-haired elf, wearing the exquisite gold and silver robes of an elven court courier, to enter the room.

"Master Deramar," he says, bowing his head to the human. "His Royal Highness the King of Reatha will see you now." Turning he exits the room followed closely by Deramar.

Making their way down a hall, covered with vines sprouting gold, silver, red, blue, and purple leaves, they make their way to a large arboretum set in the heart of the Leonessa tree. Though the tree was hollow, it had grown this way, seemly in design by the goddess of nature for the purpose of housing the elven government, who would have never hollowed out a tree for any reason.

A glowing ball of yellow-orange magic floats in the air, providing synthetic sunlight to the growing life below. Rainbow-colored birds and butterflies dance throughout the branches of oaks, pine, elm, and maple trees set in a grove around a thirty-foot tall statue of Leonessa, standing at the center of the arboretum. Encircling the grove is a wide swath of apple, pear, orange, plum, and peach trees, their blossoms flittering through the air like scented snowflakes. Circling these are a myriad assortment of nut trees. Rabbits, deer, squirrels, and other assorted docile creatures, including a pair of unicorns, wander the garden nibbling on the plants and fruits planted for their benefit as well as the elves. Surrounding the garden is a wide sky blue pond, where ducks and swans paddle lazily upon its tranquil waters and rainbow-colored fish swim within its crystalline depths.

Crossing a vine bridge over the water, they make their way along a moss-covered path. Winding their way through the garden, they cross another bridge which brings them to the other side of the arboretum. Where an elevator, formed into the likeness of a golden birdcage, waits for them.

Stepping into the elevator the elf waves his hand in front of a blue-lighted panel, causing the elevator to begin its ascent. Passing a number of crescent-shaped balconies, which sweep around to embrace the elevator, they come to a stop on the tenth floor, giving Deramar a breathtaking view of the garden below him. Stepping off the elevator they continue down another vine-covered hallway.

Passing a number of smaller halls, which branch off from the main hallway, they come to a set of double doors made from etched, smoke-colored glass. Depicted on the doors is a scene of Peramadon, the great elven hero and first king of the Light Elves, slaying the evil black dragon Dagoth with his holy spear Ansalor, given to him by Leonessa herself.

Standing before the doors, at attention, were Rait and Temar. As Deramar and the elf approach Temar turns to open the doors.

"Deramar." Rait says, nodding towards the human. "His Highness is expecting you. Go on in." Temar turns back from the doors, returning to his position of attention, while the elderly elf heads back down the hall.

Entering the room, Deramar notices it was designed more for the comfort of humans than elves. Tapestries depicting various heroic deeds, instead of plant life, cover the walls on either side of a balcony.

Thick, colorful rugs cover the floors, replacing the soft loam which is found in all the elven rooms. Couches, tables, and chairs are much thicker and appear much sturdier than the delicate, yet equally strong, furniture of elven design.

Captain Dyrgen lounges in a chair with his feet thrust out and crossed in front of him, laughing a deep, heavy, belly laugh at the antics of his king tickling his daughter on the carpet before him. As Deramar enters, the captain rises from his chair wiping white flecks of foam from his thick mustache deposited there by the mug of ale clasped within his thick, meaty fingers.

"Your Majesty may I present Deramar of Pasadera," he says, setting the mug down on a table next to him.

Rising from the floor the king sweeps his child up by the waist tosses her in the air where she spins around. Snatching her out of the air he kisses her forehead and places her back on the floor. "Daddy needs to talk to this man for a while sweetie. Do you want to play the garden for a while?"

"Yes, Daddy." She replies, smiling with pleasure at her father.

"O.K., you go tell Rait I said to take you down to the garden, so you can play," the king says, gently slapping her on the bottom as she runs off giggling. Before she can make it out of the room he stops her, "And don't throw sticks at the ducks."

His mocking is given away by the huge grin that splits his face as she throws her hands on her tiny hips, pouts her lips, and replies, "Oh pooh, Daddy. You know I don't throw stuff at the animals." And out she goes, followed by her father's profuse, roaring laughter.

As the door closes and the king turns to face him. Deramar starts to drop to one knee. Waving a hand in a decisive gesture the king addresses the newcomer. "Pah, we're not in court, so there is no need for formalities. Rise: Dyrgen here told me what you did for my family." Walking up to Deramar the king clasps his shoulder and looks him square in the eyes. "Thank you! Thank you very much." Dropping his hand indicates a chair next to where the captain was sitting. "Will you please be seated?"

Turning he goes over to a table with a decanter of wine, a pitcher of ale, and an assortment of crystal goblets and mugs. "Would you like something to drink?"

Sitting down in the chair next to Dyrgen, who once again has claimed his seat. "Thank you, your Majesty, wine please."

Filling a goblet with the bright red elven wine, Talric hands it to Deramar and then takes his seat across from them. "Captain Dyrgen told me about your plight and family. I am truly sorry for your loss." His eyes drop for a moment as he shakes his head.

Looking back up he speaks again. "I met Prince Andrus once when he was a young man. I found him to be very intelligent and wise. He would have made a fine king. We've never been able to figure out how Prince Fairinan gained such support, but we figure he must of had outside help from somewhere."

Talric stops to down his wine before continuing. "But that is not why I summoned you here. First and foremost I wanted to thank you for helping to save my daughter's life. The elf's examined that dagger you returned with. Other than determining that they came from the assassins guild in Passail, they were not able to find out anything else."

Setting his empty goblet down he leans forward. "Secondly, I have a proposal for you. Captain Dyrgen told me how you handled yourself back in the woods." Leaning forward he points a finger at Deramar. "I could use a man like you. Especially right now." Sitting back he refills his goblet and takes a sip, allowing the cool, refreshing liquid to run down his throat.

"Eminence Jerilith, Principal Citizen Steelstone, and I are putting together a small reconnaissance mission. Dyrgen thinks you would be an asset to this group." Rising from the chair he walks over to the balcony, surveying the elven city. Turning from the balcony he again turns his steely blue eyes on Deramar. "I'm not your king, so I can not order you to go. And even if I was, I wouldn't. This is strictly a volunteer mission. So the choice is yours."

Going over to a desk, set in a comer, he opens a drawer and removes a rolled-up piece of parchment with the royal seal of

Reatha stamped in wax holding it closed. "I had this writ made up for you. Present it at the royal palace in Reatha. It entitles you to five-thousand gold Rethars and five hundred acres of land." Walking over to Deramar he hands him the rolled-up piece of parchment. "These are yours if you decide to go or not."

Taking the document from the king, Deramar places it in his lap. "You are too generous your Majesty. I was only doing what I thought was right."

"It is a very small price to pay for my daughter's life," Talric replies, dismissing Deramar's humility.

Picking up his goblet, Deramar rolls it between his hands contemplating the king's request. After a moment's silence, he speaks. "If you don't mind me asking. What are we to be looking for and where is it we are supposed to go?"

"Then what," he answers. "Is what you need to determine. As for the where and the other details, they will be released to you and the others later. That is of course if you decide to go."

Deramar stares off into the gently swirling wine cupped between the palms of his hand. Breaking his gaze with the wine, he sets the goblet down on the table next to him and rises to his feet. "I accept." He says with a nod of his head. "I don't believe I'm the settling down type anymore. At least not yet."

"Great! Great!" Says Dyrgen leaping to his feet, a large smile dividing the red hair on his face, as he slaps the thin man on the back nearly sending him stumbling across the room.

"Good!" Says the king, smiling through his salt and pepper beard. Though in his late fifties he was still a powerful figure of a man. "Tomorrow all the parties shall be assembled so we can go over the details. Till then though why don't you enjoy the hospitality of the elves? I'm sure the Captain here will be more than happy to show you around."

"Of course your highness. It would be my pleasure." Replies the burly, red-bearded knight with a huge grin. "By your leave your Majesty," Dyrgen says with a bow as he and Deramar leave the king's presence.

Sitting back down, Talric picks back up his wine. The last thing the king hears before the doors close behind Dyrgen and Deramar, is the Captain of his Guard saying, "These elves' act as if they have sticks shoved so far up their asses, that it seems to give them a case of persistent constipation. But if we search hard enough we just might find a place where a couple of humans can have a decent time."

Talric shakes his head and mumbles into his graying beard. "Maximus, please don't let them start a war."

IV

Awaking to a throbbing headache and a black eye, Dyrgen arises from his bed and throws cold water on his face from a small fount flowing from the wall into a catch basin beneath it.

"Shit!" He says looking at his eye in the mirror, "That little bastard sure does hit hard," remembering the dwarf that he had gotten into a fight with last night. Leaving their audience with the king, he and Deramar had stopped to pick up Darl, then headed off into the city to apparently, he thinks rubbing his sore eye, to find trouble.

The night had started off well enough. Passing a few taverns with the sweet, monotonous, plinking sound of elfish music issuing from them, which was defiantly not the type of places they were looking for. They then came upon a place with the sound of raunchy dwarven drinking songs coming from out the windows. Entering the establishment they found it nearly empty, except for three dwarfs and what appeared to be a very stressed barkeep and flustered waitress.

Throwing his arms around the shoulders of his two companions, Dyrgen smiles. "They might not be humans but they for damn sure ain't elves." Walking into the bar he adds, "Don't get me wrong, I don't have anything against elves, but they tend to be stuck-up. I really believe they think their shit don't stink." The last part overheard by the barkeep earns him a scathing glance. "Now dwarfs, they know how to live."

Strolling up to the table with the singing dwarfs who are completely out-of-sync with each other, possibly due to the fact that they are working on their tenth round of ale, Dyrgen asks with a huge affable grin on his face. "Do you fine gentlemen mind if a few wayward humans join your group?"

"Youse buying human?" Asks one of the brawny dwarfs, wearing plate mail, a one-horned helm, and a giant mithral ax slung across his back, almost as long as he was tall.

Reaching into a pouch hanging from his belt, Dyrgen removes a handful of gold pieces and tosses them onto the table. "I believe this might get us all piss drunk."

Eyeing the gold, with the critical eye of a dwarf, then the giant red-bearded human towering over them, they first scowl then burst out laughing, slapping the table and upsetting a couple of empty mugs sitting on the table. "That it just might be human. Youse and yours' friends'es can join us'es. Seeing how there are no elves with enough balls to drink with uses."

Pulling up chairs, the three humans join the three dwarfs. Scooping up the coins, Dyrgen calls over the waitress. "Bring us six mugs of your best ale, and keep them coming till we're laying in our puke."

Scrunching her face up in disgust she snatches the coins out of Dyrgen's hand as if even touching the loutish human might contaminate her somehow, she goes behind the bar returning shortly with their order.

At some point in the night, he believes after his eleventh or twelfth mug he's not sure which, things got blurry. Something was said about Maximus and Xax, then he and the one-horned dwarf were at each other's throats, like the two brawl-loving heavenly brothers.

Then a vague recollection of the elven guard showing up, followed by awaking to this throbbing headache and black-eye.

"Shit." He says again looking at his eye. "I didn't even get the little bastard's name."

He wipes off his face and beard with a towel, made from some sort of plant fibers, suspended from a vine growing out of the wall by the basin. Leaving the mirror he goes over to a wooden stickfigure mannequin, which supports his armor. Polished and shining brilliantly, all the dents, gashes, and scars acquired in the battle of the woods are now gone and repaired by the highly-skilled elven armorers. Examining the suit of armor, he runs his fingers over the places it was damaged. Nodding his head in approval. "Not bad, not bad at all," he says grudgingly.

A sharp rapping at the door reawakens the pounding in his head, which had finally started to subside.

"What in all the hells do you want?" He growls fiercely, the closest he can manage to a yell without his head exploding and covering the room with his mush-filled brains, and throws open the door.

"Your breakfast, sir," replies a startled elf, holding a silver tray with a covered platter and a steaming pot of tea. Momentarily taken aback, by the hostility flung at him by the hung-over knight, the elf takes a half-step back. Regaining his composure, the breakfastbearing elf squares his shoulders and waits for the black-eyed Dyrgen to allow him admittance.

Mumbling something about rabbit food for breakfast, Dyrgen steps back to allow the elf into the room.

Walking to a small table, set in the center of the room, the elf places the tray down and turns to face the human. "I was instructed to tell you that the assembly will be ready for you in an hour and a half."

Picking up a cup, from off the tray, the elf pours the steaming liquid from the pot into it and hands it to Dyrgen. "This will help with your hangover," the disgust barely concealed in his voice. Elves consider drunkenness a sign of weakness, and it is an extremely rare thing to find one in that condition.

"I'm not hung-over!" Dyrgen retorts, clutching his head at his own raised voice.

"Uh-huh," replies the elf through the side of his mouth. "Anyway, I shall return in forty-five minutes to help you in to your armor." With that said he walks across the room, exits, and leaves Dyrgen to his breakfast and misery.

As the door closes, Dyrgen goes over to the table with the platter of food sitting upon it. Lifting the cover he finds to his amazement that the platter is filled to brimming over with pancakes, scrambled eggs with cheese, bacon, ham, sausage, and four pieces of toasted elven bread. "Humm," he says sitting down to eat. "They must have a human held hostage in their kitchen somewhere." He then commences devouring the food and tea, which he also found pleasing to his palate.

Finishing his breakfast, he kicks his feet up onto the table, lights a pipe, and blows smoke-rings while finishing off the pot of tea. Having a light, yet full-bodied flavor he finds the drink has indeed removed the throbbing ache that was crashing within his head.

As the last of the smoke rises above his now quiet head, he taps the ashes out onto the empty platter. Rising he crosses over to a large oak and iron-bound chest. Opening it he removes the thick padded jerkin and breeches, which keeps his armor from chafing his skin, and a blue and silver tunic emblazoned with the royal symbol of Reatha. Tossing them onto the unmade bed, he closes the chest and begins to don the breeches.

A knock comes from the door just as he finishes tying the drawstrings around his waist. "Enter!" He yells while reaching for the padded jerkin.

The door opens, letting in the elf that had brought his breakfast to him earlier. "I've come to help you with your armor and lead you to the assembly." He states brusquely with the same barely-disguised disgust look in his eyes.

"Well, isn't that mighty *human* of you?" Dyrgen retorts sardonically, getting sick of the elf's 'better that thou' attitude.

The elf's face starts to go red, as the blood rushes to his head in anger, at the implied insult. "Look," says Dyrgen, breathing out a deep sigh. "It's obvious you don't like me. I couldn't give a flying shit. You were sent here to do a job. I didn't ask for you, but here you are. So, why don't stuff your attitude and just give me a hand getting into my armor. Then you can lead me to the assembly and we can be done with each other, O.K?" The glare coming from the knight's eyes informs the elf that if the answer is not O.K. this could very well be the start of a diplomatic incident, knowing that the elves would not be pleased if he broke one of their brethren's neck in the royal palace; not to mention King Talric would probably have his skin.

Thirty minutes later Dyrgen follows the elf through the living hallways to the meeting, dressed in his newly repaired and gleaming armor, plumed helm in the crook of his arm, and sword strapped to his side. Not having said a word to each other, besides discussing the fitting and adjustment of the armor, they just nod at each other upon reaching the door to the assembly.

The door to the assembly is a large golden wood door, with two splendidly garbed and armored elven warriors standing at attention to either side. The guard to the left raps upon the door with the haft of his spear, without removing his eyes from the hallway, as the knight approaches. As the echo from his third, and final, knock fades the door opens, revealing an elf dressed in the robes of a court scribe.

"Sir Dyrgen please come in. Everybody is here or will be shortly." Stepping to the side, he motions for the knight to enter.

Entering the small room, he finds it to be an anti-chamber with a set of double-doors in the ivy-covered wall before him. Standing there are Deramar and Darl, waiting for him and admittance into the meeting. The scribe makes his way past the three humans and to the double doors.

Beckoning them to follow he opens the doors and announces, "The Knights of Reatha." Stepping to the side he motions for them to enter the main chamber.

"Be seated men." King Talric says, indicating three empty chairs beside him, set around a large circular table. As Deramar takes his seat, his eyes scan the nine figures already sitting at the table. King Talric, whom Deramar of course already knows, sits with his kinsmen. Next is Eminence Jerilith with three other elves, two men and one female, who are dressed in robes with various pouches tied around her waist, Deramar surmises must be a mage. After them are three dwarfs, sitting with Principal Citizen Steelstone. His eyes open slightly in surprise as he notices the three stocky, mail-clad figures are the same dwarfs from the night before. The face of one them, Deramar can't remember if he caught any of their names, but the one with the onehorned helm; splits into a huge grin, showing two missing teeth, as his eyes fall on the black-eyed Dyrgen. Who returns the cheerful grin with one of his own, plus adds a wink with his purplish swollen eye.

After everyone has been seated, Eminence Jerilith rises from his seat and addresses the gathered assembly. "You have all volunteered for this mission without knowing what is required of you, except for perhaps the dwarfs." He nods his thin, elegant head towards the thick, squat warriors. "But before we explain what is required from you, I would ask that each of you rise and give your name. So your compatriots will not be forced to address you as just elf, human, or dwarf." The tiniest touch of a smile raises the corners of his mouth. Retaking his seat he indicates that the elf next to him should begin.

And in this manner did Deramar learn the names of his companions, for the upcoming trek through The Northern Watse. The representatives for the elves were Elstar, the same elf that had met them on the road to Stalora, Mizzan, and Vesalin, a female mage of the first circle, who were also brother and sister and the children of Eminence Jerilith.

The dwarves, each standing in their turn were Grundel, Crundor and then rising to his feet and slamming a sledgehammer like a fist against his steel-encased chest the last dwarf proudly proclaims, "Is' is Vorrax, High Guard of the Golden Vein!" Nodding his bearded head towards Dyrgen, he flashes a smile that might be shy a few teeth but held immense joy at the sight of the barrel-chested human, knowing that, other than his fellow kinsmen, here was someone with the heart of a lion that he would be proud to spill blood with. Other than the blood they spilled, of each other, last night.

Following the dwarves were the humans, Deramar and Darl, who is a man of action and not words seemed as if giving his name was more information than he really cared to admit about himself; and finally Dyrgen rises and address the group, "Captain Dyrgen commander of the Knights of Reatha." smiling and nodding towards Vorrax.

King Talric and Principal Citizen Steelstone both look at each other and smile, now understanding why both their champions look the worst for wear this morning.

After the introductions, Eminence Jerilith rises to his feet. "Now that we all have been introduced, though I do believe that some of you have already met." His twinkling eyes dart to Dyrgen and Vorrax, showing that he hadn't missed the exchange between the two warriors. "I shall turn the meeting over to the Principal Citizen." Motioning towards the dwarven leader he retakes his seat.

Kash Steelstone rises to face the gathered group with a dour expression on his already gruff features. He begins by relating the same tale of woe that befell the lost groups and the cryptic words 'dark forces' that were uttered by the dying dwarf. After relating the pathetically little information they had the Principal Citizen retakes his seat. A moment of silence befalls the group as the scant information and what it might mean sink in.

Finally, Jerilith rises again. "It seems clear," he begins, going over to a map of Tamora hanging on the wall." That something or someone has stirred up the dark creatures of the north. For over a thousand years the north has been guarded by the power and might of Xaxtor. I do not doubt that the dwarves can stop and destroy any force that is thrown at Xaxtor," he adds this last part not only because he believes it true, but also to soothe the wounded pride of the dwarves----"Who in that thousand years have never asked for assistance in protecting their homeland." Seeing the dwarves' eyes lift and chests swell, he knows his words had their desired effect. "But anything that can instill such fear in the stout heart of a dwarf, and cause him to age at such an alarming rate is of grave concern for us all. And because of this the nine of you have been recruited."

Reaching up to the map, he taps a finger indicating the entrance to Xaxtor. "You will first go with PrincipaJ Citizen Steelstone back to his kingdom, learning if any new information has come from The Northern Waste. From there you are to enter the wastelands. Here let me be very clear." His eyes scan the gathered group. "You are a reconnaissance party. You are not to engage with whatever you find there unless you are attacked. I emphasize this because if there is an army gathering, we do not want them alerted till we have time to gather our forces."

"After you have determined what these 'dark forces' consist of, you are to return to Xaxtor so we can determine our next course of action." Turning to Talric and Kash, he asks, "Do either one of you have anything you wish to add?"

Both leaders shake their heads indicating that Jerilith has covered everything. "In that case," the elf continues to the group, "Do any of you have any questions?"

Dyrgen arises, "Yes, I have a question. Do we know the path or perhaps the location where the dwarves encountered this 'dark force'?"

Jerilith nods towards Kash, indicating he should answer this question. "Wees' don't know the exact location, but wees' do have a general idea. Wees' have maps in Xaxtor that hold more detail of The Northern Waste, than these here. When wees' get back to Xaxtor, wees' will go over them with youse."

"Are there any more questions?" Jerilith asks the group again. He's answered only by silence and the intent looks of the group. "In that case, you leave in an hour. Everything has been prepared. You will find all your gear and horses waiting for you below. I wish you all luck and return safe to us with the information we require to combat this menace."

V

The crashing of a chair, followed by a bellowing roar of outrage, punctuates the pandemonium and ruckus-filled tavern.

Rising in outrage, from an ale-stained table, an orc grabs the goblin that offended him by its scrawny neck, preparing to smash his pleading, bulbous face in the solid black oak table. He pauses as the front door to the tavern opens, also made from the same black oak with a crimson skull emblazoned on it, letting in the raging storm which is quickly followed by a cloaked figure, who closes the door to the smoke-filled establishment.

Letting the goblin slip from his limp fingers, which quickly runs off to a dark corner rubbing its neck, the orc leers in lust as the figure removes her hood. Hiding beneath the soaked woolen garment stands a gorgeous dark-elf female. Reaching behind her ivory white neck, she frees her hair from the cloak letting her raven-black tresses fall down her back past her waist. Scanning the crowd with her emerald eyes she spies an empty stool at the bar.

Deftly making her way through the jeering crowd, seductively dodging the hands' thrust towards her, she reaches the empty stool at the bar. Preparing to sit she is interrupted as a human, with rotting teeth and the look of a petty thief about him swoops upon her.

"Heyyy, baby. Canns l buysss you sssomething?" He asks placing his hand on her rear, his words so slurred that she can barely understand him.

Putting on her sweetest smile, the elven maiden rubs her hand up to his cheek and behind his neck. Then kicking his feet out from under him, she slams his face into the scared bar top. The crack that resounds from the encounter causes the tavern to go momentarily quiet and the unfortunate thief to slump lifelessly to the sawdust, vomit, and urine-covered floor.

"I told that dumb-shit that some bitch would put him in his place one day." Someone in the crowd states, followed by a roaring bout of laughter throughout the tavern. The clientele then turns back to their own business, except for an ogre who appears to work for the place. Walking over he grabs the would-be Casanova by a leg and drags him out the back, to be thrown on the refuse pile with the rest of the garbage to be picked over by the rats and crows.

Leaving his place by a huge open hearth, located in the center of the room, a dark-dwarf, with a metal patch riveted over one eye, orders a goblin servant to take over the basting of some sort of creature which the woman has never seen before. Shoving his way through the drunken mass he makes his way behind the bar to the place in front of the elf.

With sweat running down his bald head and shaven cheeks, he wipes his greasy hands on an even greasier apron and asks. "So sweetness, what's your poison?"

"Candilyne Brandy." Her sweet, honeyed voice responds.

"Candilyne Brandy! Candilyne Brandy her lordship wants!" He bellows, throwing his arms wide in the air, talking to everyone and no one at the same time. "You kill one of my patrons and then order the most expensive drink in all of Tamora. Who do you think you are?" His voice is all business, as he squints his one good eye up at the woman. "Do you know how much Candilyne Brandy cost?"

Reaching into her dripping cloak the dark-elf female withdraws a small ruby and places it on the grimy bar top. "This should cover it."

As soon as the first gleam bounces off the shimmering crimson surface, a fat grubby hand sweeps out and snatches the jewel off the bartop and tucks it away.

"Ah!" He says with a smile. "The lady does know the cost of a good drink." Laughing to himself he adds. "That filth did not." Indicating the back door with a thumb, from which the ogre is now returning.

Heading towards the back, He quickly returns wiping off a bottle that is covered in dust. Following him is a human servant girl wiping a glass with what appears to be a clean rag, and from the look of the place, probably the only one in the tavern. Placing the bottle in front of the elf, he turns and takes the clean glass, now with greasy fingerprints on it, from the servant girl and places it next to the bottle.

"If you need anything you just let me know. I'm Dagith One-eye and I own the Crimson Skull." Thumping his barrel chest he indicates himself, then throwing his arms wide he indicates his tavern." The best damn tavern in all of Passail. Food should be ready in about thirty minutes." He nods his bald, sweaty head towards the roasting beast.

Through strange in appearance, the delicious aroma arising from the hearth sets the woman's stomach to rumble.

Smiling Dagith pats his rotund belly. "I'll have it brought out to the lady as soon as it is ready. Will the lady be needing a room for the night? I have my best room available." He waves an arm towards a staircase off to the side.

"Oh, your best room is it?" She says, smiling at the dark-dwarf and downing her first glass of the glowing amber liquid, which the servant girl had poured after re-wiping the glass.

"Aye, my lady, fit for nobility it is." The dwarf says feigning an injured pride, at the implied notion that he was not offering her his best room. "I always keep the best room available for the highest bidder. If you know what I mean?" Winking his one good eye he crosses his arms across his greasy hairless chest.

Pouring herself another drink she asks, "And what if I'm not the highest bidder?" Locking her emerald eyes onto his one exposed brown eye, she downs her drink. "What then?"

Something about her gaze sends a cold wave pulsing through his body. Having had to face rowdy orcs, ogres, and other unsavory characters, not to mention breaking a few heads in his fifty years of owning the Crimson Skull, nothing had made him feel like she just did. As if his heart had just stopped and jumped into his throat.

As the shiver finishes running down his spine, he swallows the lump in his throat. "Miss…" He begins rather subdued. "I haven't had anyone pay close to what you just paid. Besides," he adds, shaking his head and gathering some of his bolstered back. "I like you! Why? I don't know. There is something about you that excites me."

"Oh, it does?" She seductively runs an elegantly nailed finger under his second chin.

"Ah, Ha-Ha-Ha!" The dwarf laughs slapping one arm down on the bartop, nearly upsetting the expensive bottle of brandy.

Pointing his finger at the sexy female elf he laughs again. "I'm not like this scum." He indicates the drunken louts in the tavern. "Ready to pounce on anything with a heartbeat." He leans forward as if to tell her something confidential. "I'm not too damn sure that many of them care about the heartbeat." Pulling back from her he thumps his chest and boasts loudly. "I like my women with a little more meat on their bones. Elf women are too bony, they bruise easily. If you get my meaning? Laughing at his wit he slaps his arm back down upon the bar.

The elf woman's hand shoots out catching the bottle and keeping it from turning over before the servant girl even has a chance to react to the mishap.

"Well then, what about that room? You want it?" Dagith asks, recomposing himself.

Pouring herself another drink, the elf replies. "I'll let you know later. But I will have some of that which you are cooking. What is it?" She inquires almost innocently.

Cocking his good eye at her, he thinks at first she is having fun with him. Then he realizes that she doesn't know what it is. "It's beef, my lady. Have you never seen beef before?"

"Beef, huh? Yes, I'll have some beef." She says eyeing the roasting beef lustfully.

"Well then, I'll have it sent over as soon as it is ready. And you let me know about that room, O.K. But don't take too long. "The last part is said over his shoulder. Heading back through the crowd to relieve the goblin, which he chastises for turning the spit too fast.

Turning around to face the drunken rabble, Dak'tari smiles to herself. "If everything goes as well as it has so far, I'll be able to retrieve the Fingerbone of Gauntlar sooner than I hoped."

*****

After leaving the members of the Brotherhood on the shores of Traxess, Dak'tari made her way inland through the black and haunting forest which makes up the dark-elves homeland. Where the light- elves guide and nurture nature, the dark-elves force and manipulate nature into doing their bidding, leaving the woods a spiteful and oppressive place.

Traveling for what she guessed must have been about two days, for the canopy of the dark forest never let in the sunlight, keeping the forest floor in an eerie dead stillness, the gnarled branches of the trees forbade entry into their domain by the sun or wind. Dak'tari thrills at the creaking boughs and snapping twigs, caused by only the gods know what creatures, which would have frozen the hearts of even the most stout-hearted men. Throwing her arms to the tree-shrouded heavens, exhilarated she spins slowly, reveling in her newfound freedom. Her first time alone, she finally feels truly alive. Tossing back her head she laughs, as she never has in her short life, to be answered by a storm ripping apart the sky above her and the dark canopy.

The sound of cursing and creaking wagon wheels snaps her back to reality. Spinning she focuses on the sound. Heading towards the southeast she comes upon a road with what appears to be a dark-elf caravan making its way towards her.

Pulling up quickly on the reins of his horse, the lead rider stops to keep from running over the cloaked figure that has just stepped into his path.

Drawing the scimitar from his side, as the two riders behind him raise their crossbows, he orders. "Halt! Who are you? Show yourself and state your business!" He approaches the figure in the road slowly, ready to split their skull if they mean harm to his caravan.

Removing her hood, Dak'tari stands before the guard as a beautiful dark-elf female.

"Sorry, sir." She replies demurely. "I'm on my way to Passail." She stands with her arms wrapped around herself, trembling from the rain which has started to make its way through the thick canopy.

"What in all the hells is the hold-up!" A dark-elf in exquisite black chainmail barks. Riding up at a gallop, his horse kicks mud on Dak'tari as it skids to a halt in the wet mud of the road. "Who the *hell are you? And what are you doing on this road?" He demands, scrutinizing Dak'tari.*

Looking up at him Dak'tari realizes he would be very handsome if not for the permanent scowl etched upon his features. His hair was jet black, pulled back in a ponytail, and slick with the fresh rain. Sitting straight back and arrogant in the saddle, his deep violet eyes swallow her emerald ones in their gaze.

'Yes. 'She thinks. 'He is quite pleasing to the eye.' Laughing to herself she adds, 'Oh yes, you will do nicely.'

"Answer me, wench!" He exclaims as the rain starts to pour even heavier through the trees. "Are you deaf?"

"She says she is hea.." The first rider starts.

"Did I ask you?" The apparent leader turns on him, cutting him off.

"My name is Tanara, and I need to get to Passail. Can you help me please?" She says this while pulling the cloak even tighter around her shoulders, and allowing her shivering to become more pronounced.

"Why in all the hells do I need a girl slowing up my caravan?" He asks, preparing to order his men to ride on and leave the girl behind in the rain.

Before he can give the order or spur his horse on, Dak'tari replies in her most seductive voice. A voice that would melt butter in the dead of winter. "I'm not as much of a girl as you might think."

Turning back he finds that she has turned her head up into the rain. All traces of her earlier chills are gone, she is massaging her neck and letting the rain run down her face, neck, and heaving ivory white cleavage, which is nearly bursting out of her blouse. Turning her face back down from the flowing rain, she shakes out her waist-length black hair, causing the horse to prance skittishly.

"So your just going to leave me out here, by myself, in what appears to be a long cold night?" She purrs, raising her emerald eyes pleadingly while running her thin, smooth hand up to his leg.

"Ha, perhaps you will be worth taking along." The scowl being replaced with a lustful leer. Reaching down he grabs Dak'taris waiting

arm and pulls her up behind him. Smiling to herself she wonders if all males are so easy.

"We'll make camp about a mile ahead." He tells his men. Then turning towards Dak'tari he adds, rubbing her exposed thigh next to him. "Then we will see if you are worth taking to Passail."

"Oh, I'm worth it. Trust me." She whispers to him, pressing her face into his back while rubbing his crotch.

✶✶✶✶✶

Four days later Dak'tari sits on the bar stool in The Crimson Skull. She had used her time with Sameron, the leader of the caravan, satisfying his beastly urges while plying him for all the information she could get about Passail.

Raising her glass in a solo salute, she says "This ones for you, Sameron." And then downing the glass of warm amber fluid, smiling a crooked little grin as if she knows a secret that the rest of the room is not privy to, she thinks. *I guess they should be finding what remains of you by tomorrow.*

It was through her questioning of Sameron that Dak'tari had learned of The Crimson Skull. At her 'innocent, benign' questioning he had mentioned that a priest of Gauntlar came here quite often. It was he that she now waited on.

After watching the crowd for a few minutes, while keeping an eye on the door, Dak'tari notices Dagith making his way towards her with a large steaming platter of roast beef. Pouncing on the plate of food as soon as the dark-dwarf sets it down, who jumps back at the surprising ferocity with which the demure-looking elf tears into the food, and for the fear of possibly losing an arm or finger to the blinding speed of the jabbing fork and slicing knife.

Watching her devour the food as if she hadn't eaten in weeks, a beaming smile of pride stretches the dwarf's features. "So, you like it, huh?"

Only half lifting her eyes from the now half-gone platter she nods her head once and continues her feeding frenzy. Having never tasted beef, her diet up to that point had consisted of nothing but fish, rabbit, birds, and a few vegetables that grew on the island. The beef, with its dripping blood, was the nectar of the gods to her.

Finishing off her meal, by sopping up the blood-stained gravy with a piece of black bread, she wipes her grease-covered fingers on her half-dry cloak. Sliding the platter away from her, she leans back and rubs her full belly with a very sated look on her face.

"So will there be anything else for her ladyship?" The dwarf asks, picking up the near spotless platter and wiping the bar top with the greasy apron around his waist.

"No, that will be all." She replies while turning towards the door, which has just opened, letting in the man she has been waiting on.

The priest, with his head shaved and face painted to represent a skull, steps into the room and closes the door to the storm raging behind him. His robe, open to the waist showing the deep scars that run along his ribs, shows him to be a Balsafar, the highest order of priest under the high priest of Gauntlar himself.

So, she smiles, *Sameron information was correct.*

"Yes, I'll take that room now," she tells the dwarf, her eyes never once leaving the priest.

"It will be ready in a few minutes." He replies, slapping a goblin servant in the back of its head, speeding it off to make the room ready. Meanwhile, his eyes flick back and forth from Dak'tari to the priest. You didn't run a tavern-like The Crimson Skull in Passail for fifty years and did not realize when something was up. But he also knew you didn't live fifty years to run a tavern-like The Crimson Skull by getting involved unless absolutely necessary.

"Oogie will bring you your key when the room is ready." Walking back to the hearth he hopes this is not going to cost him too much in damages.

Keeping her eyes on the priest as he makes his way through the throng, she watches as the crowd parts before him as if scared to be touched by him or even brush against his robes. Heading for a table in the back, shadowed corner, the occupants fleeing as they notice his destination, he sits and waits in stony silence watching the crowd slowly get back to normal.

The servant girl, which had kept Dak'tari's glass clean, rushes to the table with a platter of the beef and a bottle of red wine. Setting them down on the table she slides them towards him, as if afraid to get too close.

From the information she extracted from Sameron last night, which had not been nearly as gentle as the previous nights but was infinitely more pleasing for her, this should be Balsafar Ekthar. Though not required to be celibate, on the contrary, it was encouraged for them to have sex and spread the venereal diseases they were sure to carry, and as they like to put it 'spread the blessing of their lord,' but being followers of the Lord of Disease it was only the very drunk, very stupid or the very devout that consented to go to bed with one of them. But 'talking' to Sameron, she knows that that will not work with this one - Balsafar's weak spot was converts, and that was how she planned to ensnare him.

As Oogie brings Dak'tari the key to her room, she tucks it into her cloak and makes her way across the tavern towards the priest.

"Balsafar Ekthar, may I speak with you?" She asks, reverting to her 'little lost elf girl' voice. "Sameron said you should be the one I talk to."

Glaring up from his meal, Ekthar's gravelly voice spoken at a near whisper carries easily over the din to Dak'tari's finely pointed elvin ears. "Who are you and how do you know Sameron?"

Squaring her shoulder's she looks at the skeletal painted face hiding in the shadows. "I am Tanara Estalar," she says, bowing in reverence towards the Balsafar. "I was traveling towards the temple of our lord Gauntlar." She bows her head forward, crosses her hands over her chest, then raises them to cover her face, and finally drops them back down to cross over her chest again in the sign of supplication to the god of death. "When Sameron's caravan came upon me on the road to Passail."

Leaning forward from the shadows, Balsafar sets his goblet of wine down upon the table. "And what is it you want from me?" Placing his elbows on the scarred table, he gazes more intently upon the dark-elf standing before him, his interest peaked over the small act of devotion she performed to his deity. Which Dak'tari had figured would be a nice touch.

Dropping to her knees she grabs the filthy hem of the drab gray robes, gently touching them to her lips. As she kisses the hem, she looks up with pleading eyes. "I want to be a priestess of Gauntlar, my lord."

A grotesque smile splits the skeletal painted face, revealing that all his teeth have been pulled giving him an even move skeletal aspect. His eyes start to flicker with a fanatic fervor, then simmer down as he squints upon the girl kneeling before him. "Why?"

Remaining on her knees, she looks up at him. "Four months ago a plague swept through my town.."

"What town?" The priest interrupts.

"Thasal." She answers immediately. Another piece of information she had extracted from Sameron. Knowing that every good lie had to have some verifiable information contained within it.

The priest visibly eases, a part of his suspicions alleviated by the fact that indeed a town named Thasal was indeed struck by the cleansing hand of his god four months ago.

Continuing, her voice starts to rise in a sort of religious ecstasy. "At first as the plague swept through the town I was terrified. The number of my people dying was horrific, my parents and my brother died within the first few weeks. Our clerics and mages tried to halt the plague, but they succumbed to it just as readily as the rest of the population."

"As I watched everybody dying around me, I began to realize that for some reason I seemed to be immune to the plague."

"In despair, I started to curse Disatara for letting my family and people die. But as I walked through the piles of rotting corpses, lying in the streets, I began to realize who held power in the heavens. Gauntlar! Yes, it was he who had sent the plague, but it was Disatara who was impotent to stop him and save her people."

"I was to become a priestess of Disatara for my people, but I decided then that I would not serve a puny, weak goddess. I would instead serve a god who endures! A god who is forever! The god of death! Gauntlar!" As she finishes, her breast heaving with the exciting rush of her breathing, she gazes up at the priest. "So I came to Passail to devote myself to the god of death and disease."

"The fire burns bright within your eyes, I see," Ekthar replies with a fanatical fire burning within his own eyes as well. "But, are you truly worthy to serve our Lord?"

"Oh, yes Balsafar!" She pleads. "I am! I know I am! Please help me become a servant of Gauntlar! I beseech you!" She then drops her head in dejection. "What can I do to prove my worth? I have a room perhaps we can go there and talk in private? You can tell me what is required to become a priestess." She looks up again with pleading eyes.

"Are you trying to tempt me?!" His voice flares with anger.

"N..N..No Balsafar! I would never!" She recoils shocked by his fury. It was not what she expected, she had him but now she started to fear that she might have gone too far and lost him. Gathering herself she tries to mend the damage. "It was just, I thought if we could go someplace private where you might question me. You would be able to see that my intentions are true. That's all I meant, I swear." She slumps to the floor clutching his yellowed nailed, mud-covered, bare feet. Weeping false tears, which she had only shed once for real in her life.

"Stop your sniveling girl!" He demands, kicking Dak'tari off his feet. Rising he grabs her by the hair, pulling her to her feet. "Let's see if you are truly worthy enough to be accepted into the arms of Gauntlar." Dropping her hair he seizes the back of her neck and begins to guide her towards the rooms upstairs. Heading towards the stairs Dak'tari feigns supplication, while inwardly she thrills in the knowledge that she has him within her snare.

The table closest to the scene, full of dark-elves too drunk for their good, starts to spew crude comments towards the exiting priest and dark-elf.

With a wave of his free hand, a swarm of mosquitoes flows from the sleeve of his robe and descends upon the foolhardy table. Yowling with pain and misery they rush pell-mell towards the door, slapping frantically at themselves and the swarm tormenting them. As they exit the tavern in the hopes to escape the minor torment unleashed upon them by Ekthar, howls of laughter and ridicule fill the room following them, and they swarm out into the storm-filled night.

Reaching the top floor of the three-storied building, Dakt'ari leads Balsafar to a single door at the end of the hall. Removing the key from the folds of her cloak she inserts it into the lock and enters the large, plush room. Dagith had not been exaggerating when he had said the room was fit for nobility. It was rather remarkable for a place like The Crimson Skull, but then again it was the best tavern in all of Traxess.

Entering the room, Balsafar drops his hand from Dak'tari's neck so he can turn and lock the thick wooden door. As Balsafar turns back from this small task, he is greeted by a blinding flash and slumps to the ground unconscious, never realizing that it was Dak'tari's booted foot, connecting to his jaw, that put him in that state.

★★★★★

Balsafar Ekthar groggily returns back to consciousness, with an excruciating, throbbing pain in his jaw. Prying open his eyes he finds a blonde human female, with the strangest midnight blue eyes, standing over him.

Lashing out he discovers he has been stripped and bound to the bed, with the torn sheets from that same piece of furniture. Slumping back he tries to summon a prayer to punish the defiler of his person. But through the shattered jaw he is incapable of articulating the words required to strike down his captor.

A sinister grin of malicious glee spreads across Dak'tari's face as she watches the useless gibberish tumble from the broken, toothless mouth.

"Before...you...use...these...we...shall...dispatch...with...them... also" Each word is punctuated with the snap of a finger or thumb, rendering his hands useless. Rising from the broken digits the smile spreads even farther across her features.

"Now," She says, sitting down next to his scared and naked body, gently, almost tenderly, stroking his painted cheek. "You will tell me all I wish to know?" The last word is emphasized by her grasping his broken jaw and squeezing till tears of pain well up within his eyes. "Do we understand each other?" Still smiling, she rises from his side.

"Fooo oou plitch!" He spits at Dak'tari, his eyes burning with impotent fury.

"Ah." She says, with mock sadness, shaking her head. "We don't understand each other." Kissing his painted, sweating forehead, she adds. "We must fix that."

Walking over to a table, in front of a shuttered window, she removes a piece of cord that is used to tie back the curtains on either side of the window. Returning to the priest she ties the cord around his leg, just above the knee.

The anger in the Balsafar's eyes begins to shift to fear. For the forty years, since joining the priesthood, he was the one to instill fear in others. Who would not fear, where a disciple of death tread. Since the time of his initiation, he had not had to face fear, let alone feel it, feeling confident and all-powerful within the folds of his religion. But he felt it now. It was certainly not the fear of dying. He worshipped death, death would just carrying him to the arms of his waiting god. It was the dawning realization that this girl wanted something from him, something that could cause him to betray his faith. And something about her made him fear, that she just might be able to extract it from him.

He winces as she pulls the cord tight, cutting off the circulation to the lower part of his left leg. "Now," she says, drawing the black stiletto from its place at her side. "You will tell me how to reach the high priest's chambers and what I will encounter along the way."

Taking the blade she slowly cuts a thin slit completely around his leg just above his ankle. Continuing the slit she brings it up to his leg, along the shinbone, to his knee just below the knotted cord.

Where the cut meets above his ankle, she inserts her thumb-nails and begins to rip the skin loose from his muscle.

The sickening, tearing sound of the priest being skinned alive is barely drowned out by the tortured screams of agony which flees from his shattered skeletal face. Even though the screams reverberate throughout the room, even from the broken jaw, Dak'tari knows they will never carry over the clamor from the tavern. Besides even if they did no one would care.

Tearing the dangling piece of flesh from around his knee, Dak'tari flings it to the polished wooden floor, where it splats with a meaty thump, like a blood-soaked towel flung to the ground.

Reaching down, Dak'tari pats the purplish, bleeding exposed calf muscle, waking the priest from the sweet bliss of unconsciousness, having had passed out from the excruciating pain of being flayed alive.

Walking back to the curtains she removes another piece of cord from the opposite window. Tying this one below the knee of his right leg, she sweetly asks, "So, shall we continue, or are you ready to tell me what I wish to know?"

*****

Six hours later Dak'tari stands at the water basin, which Oogie had freshly poured while getting the room ready, washing the blood from her hands. As the water transforms from clear to crimson, a feeling of pride touches Dak'tari's, black heart. Quite pleased with herself and the job she has done with the mangled priest, laying on the blood-soaked bed. Sure that she has extracted all the information she requires to reach the high priest.

Returning to the bed, she looks down upon the mutilated visage that is only barely recognizable as humanoid. Having gained everything she wished to know by the time she had finished with his arms and legs, she had gone ahead and finished skinning the rest of him; partly for pleasure but mostly due to necessity. This also included his chest, to remove the tell-tale signs that he was a priest of Gauntlar.

After the removal of the skin from his body, she turned her attention to his face. Covering it in a mass of scars, making it completely unrecognizable. She then took hold of his butchered face, holding it still, as she inserted her blade into his eyes, plucking them out like olives with a toothpick. Then squeezing the shattered remnants of his jaw, she forces the mouth open and removes his tongue. Finally cutting off the broken stubs that were his thumbs.

As she steps back to survey her handy work nodding in approval, she wipes a blood-stained hand across her sweaty forehead leaving a blazing badge of horror streaked there. Removing a small blue vial from a pouch at her waist, she walks over to tenderly stroke the scalped head of the priest. "I guess you think I will kill you now?"

Her only reply is the shallow, bubbly breathing of Balsafar. Bending over, her voice thick with malice, she whispers in where his left ear should have been. "Why would I send you to that pathetic excuse of a God that you worship? So you can inform him of my plans? No, my sweet toy, that will not be the case today." Still stroking the skinless brow, the exposed flesh rippling through her fingers like some gruesome gelatin, she adds, "I have a different plan for you. Oh, you will probably die soon enough. Just not right now. I only need a little time, then I could care less what happens to you." With that said she empties the vial down his throat.

As the healing potion starts to take effect, she stands back and watches the transformation. The first noticeable effect is the easing of his ragged, gurgling breath. Then the skin starts to reform over the exposed flesh. But instead of smooth new skin, it bubbles and ripples across his body in a mass of scar tissue, leaving him looking like a blind, mute, thumbless, grotesquely scarred burn victim.

Opening the curtains and shutters, Dak'tari is greeted by the rising rays of the morning sun as it peaks its face over the rooftops of Passail. Balsafar Ekthar's head appears from the opening and scans the alleyway behind the tavern. Seeing nothing but the rats rampaging the refuse pile, with the body of the drunken thief laying on the top with part of his face missing from the rat's sharp, hungry teeth, the head withdraws back into the window. Popping back out Dak'tari, still wearing the features of Balsafar, starts tossing the mangled pieces of flesh removed from the priest onto the pile. 'Balsafar' withdraws back into the room, only to reappear shortly with the scarred lump of flesh that is Balsafar Ekthar. Dropping it from the window it, flails at the air as if trying to take flight, before landing in the pile of garbage, vomit, urine, and rotting corpses. As the scarred remnants of Balsafar disrupt the feeding frenzy of the grime-covered rats, most skitter off squealing in surprise and anger. While the braver ones turn their beady red eyes on the intruder and viciously unleash their sharp, yellow teeth on this fresh, squirming food source. As the rats commence to sink their teeth into his flesh, Balsafar Ekthar thrashes about blindly trying to dislodge the diseased-ridden vermin from his naked, mutilated body.

The back door opens to reveal the ogre bouncer, who had come out back to see what was causing all the commotion. Spotting the 'beggar' being eaten alive by the garbage pile, he lumbers over and snatches him up by the neck. Flinging him down the alley, he roars at the pathetic excuse for a human. "We don't serve beggars! You go find breakfast someplace else!"

As the 'beggar' crawls his way down the alley, blindly feeling the way before him, the ogre returns into the tavern. As he exits the back and enters the main room he has just enough time to spot Balsafar Ekthar leaving through the front door.

VI

The temple of Gauntlar stands over Passail, resembling the gargantuan upper body of a disease-riddled, emaciated corpse rising from out of a black flagstone base. The pitted white granite starts just above the hipbone, resembling the god of death tearing free from the confines of the earth. Extending one hundred and fifty feet into the air sits the carved skull, emitting a sickly purplish light from the hollow eye-sockets. Set below the sternum is the entranceway, also a skull carved as if screaming in agony.

Dak'tari, cloaked in the guise of Balsafar Ekthar, passes four temple guards dressed in white skeletal armor. They stand as stiff and erect as death itself on either side of the entrance, giving no sign of acknowledgment what-so-ever as she makes her way past them and enters the howling maw of the entranceway.

After passing through the entrance Dak'tari enters a pitch-black hallway ending about twenty yards ahead in a pale yellow light, designed to represent the dark passage from life into death.

Continuing down the 'Passageway of Death' she enters the lighted area. On the opposite side of the chamber are two spiral stairways, one leading upwards, the other down. From the information she gathered from Ekthar, the stairway going down is the main shrine used by the population of Passail to make their offerings to Gauntlar, while the one going up will lead her to the temple proper and the high priest, she begins to make her way towards the upward staircase.

Winding her way upstairs she passes a number of hallways branching off at various levels from the stairs. Ignoring all these she continues till she reaches a large chamber at the top. Located at the shoulder level of the temple, she is met by eight more guards dressed as those below, except instead of white their amour is made from red lacquered bones. Two of the guards stand at the head of the stairs she is on, while two each stand guard at the steps leading up the arms and two more before the steps leading to the skull chamber. Standing in the center of the chamber is a basin made from human bones topped with the hollowed-out skull of an ogre with the skullcap removed.

Performing the same act of supplication which she had performed for Ekthar, the guards at the top of the stairs let her pass. Walking past them she moves to stand in front of the basin, removing a small silver dagger which she had gotten from Balsafar Ekthar. As she retrieves the dagger with her left hand she acts as if she is holding the sheath with her right hand, while palming a small piece of cloth soaked in the blood of Balsafar. Holding her hand over the basin she carefully pulls the blade through her hand and across the blood-soaked rag, making sure not to draw her blood and have it contaminate the blood of the unfortunate priests. Squeezing the cloth within her hand she allows a few drops of the Balsafar's blood to drip into the skull.

As the drops of blood splatter within the rusty-colored inside of the skull, a croaking, haunting voice echoes through the chamber from the skull mounted upon the bone platform.

"Balsafar Ekthar Redalgen," the voice croaks. "You have not been summoned. What is your business here?"

"I bring news concerning a plot against our lord Gauntlar." Dak'tari responds in the voice of Ekthar.

The skull emits an eerie, hollow laugh. "Who could threaten the Lord of Death?"

"A girl, a human girl." Behind the visage of Ekthar the little girl, that is still a part of Dak'tari, fights back the glee of her truthful deceit.

"A girl! A human girl!" The voice spits with growing ire. "Is this some sort of joke? If so I am not amused!"

"No Tha'gal! I would never have come without being summoned if I didn't think she posed a threat. I know it is not proper, but I must be allowed to speak with you." She pauses waiting for a reply from the high priest. As the silence drags on she debates with herself, trying to decide if she should take this as far as she was considering. Finally deciding that the necessity of reaching the high priest outweighed caution! she adds. "I heard her mention the ancient enemy. The one we are not allowed to name."

"What!" A touch of dread spreads through the voice. "Come up! Come up, now!"

Dak'tari fights the nearly uncontrollable desire to smile, as she approaches the stairs that lead to the high priest.

Climbing the thirty black steps, she comes to a large archway made from the interlaced bones and skulls from all the races of Tamora. Set in the center of the archway is a black iron door engraved with the intricate images of tortured souls suffering from the ghastly effects of famine, pestilence, and plague. It was quite beautiful Dak'tari notices, being carved with great care and devotion.

As she reaches the door it silently swings open, emitting the sickly purplish light that issues forth from the temple skull's eye-sockets, onto the city below. Stepping through the doorway she enters the ghastly light, which blankets the inner-sanctum of the high priest.

The giant rounded room, which makes up the inside of the skull, is near bare. Sculpted upon the wall are more images of dying, disease-riddled bodies. These leap from the wall as if trapped in quicksand and frozen in time, reaching, pleading, and begging for salvation from those that pass by; only to be answered by the silent anguished screams of those trapped next to them. Hanging from the ceiling in the center of the skull, in front of the windows which make up the eye-sockets, is a huge golden brazier from which the purplish light flows. Directly below the brazier is a plain black granite throne where sits the object of Dak'tari's quest. The Fingerbone of Gauntlar, suspended from a thin silver chain, hanging around the neck of Tha'gal, high priest of Gauntlar.

Dressed in a flowing black robe with the hood draped over his face, the high priest beckons Dak'tari forward with a wave of his hand. As he makes the gesture the sleeve of his robe slips down, revealing a skeletal hand. Stepping forward, Dak'tari approaches Tha'gal, as she does he raises his head locking two glowing red eyes upon her. Fighting back her surprise Dak'tari realizes that the high priest is a lich.

Her surprise turns to anger as she realizes that Ekthar had kept that piece of information from her. *Next time, she vows. I will not be so gentle with those I interview. I will make sure I have all the required information.*

"Now what is this about the nameless one, Ekt..." The fiery eyes of the lich flash in anger as if doused with unholy fuel. "You are not Balsafar Ekthar! Who are you? And where is my priest?" He demands, rising from his throne to face Dak'tari, as the hood slips from his skull.

"How did you know?" The surprise is evident in her voice, as she drops her disguise and resumes her form.

"You have no soul, girl! I don't know how or why. But it does not matter, you shall die anyway!" Uttering the command word for death he stretches out his arm. A black inky force spews from his skeletal hand and slams into Dak'tari's chest, sending her crashing into the wall shattering one of the carved figures with her impact. Black sparks dance around Dak'tari, keeping her pinned against the wall, before dissipating and dropping her amongst the shattered remnants of the broken statue.

Though caught off guard by his spell Dak'tari quickly regains her feet and breath, which was knocked from her lungs by the impact with the wall.

"How?" Was all he could utter, his turn to be surprised. No one should have been able to survive a command of death issued from the high priest of death, much less regain their feet and get back up.

Screaming with unbridled fury, she draws her stiletto and charges the lich. Expecting it to transform into her sword, she finds a circular blade in her hand instead. Not caring what weapon she holds, she launches her attack against the high priest.

Bringing her weapon down upon his shoulder it passes right through him as if he was made of air. The unexpectedness of this development and the lack of resistance, causes her to pass through him, tumble to the ground, and crash into his throne. Momentarily at a loss, Dak'tari is struck by the bony hand of Tha'gal, sending her reeling backward to sprawl over the arm of the throne. Shocked and starting to panic, she begins to fear she might fail her beloved. Clutching her weapon she demands and then pleads for it to obey her will and become something she can fight with, but it refuses, remaining the circular blade.

Tha'gal's foot lashes out, aiming for her head. Rolling backward, she goes into a triple backflip, narrowly avoiding the bony appendage. As she comes to a halt her eye catches a gleaming flicker bouncing off the golden brazier hanging from the ceiling.

Then it dawns on her why her blade refuses to obey her will. It was trying to tell her, in its way, what she needed to do. But unfortunately, now the high priest was no longer where she needed him to be. Making his way towards her sparks begin to flicker and crackle around his flesh-less fingers.

Charging towards him, she dives as if to tackle him. Passing through his ethereal form, before he can unleash his spell, she goes into a roll. Coming to a stop by the black throne she regains her feet, faces the lich, and braces herself for the attack which she knows is coming.

Hoping that her mother's blood will divert the energy of this attack as well, for that is the only reason she can think of why his command of death might have failed, she waits. It was a risk, but she had to get him back by his throne.

White sparks flair from his hands as he brings them in front of himself, forming the shape of a diamond with his bony fingers and thumbs.

Dak'tari howls in pain as the sparkling lance of white fire smashes into her, encircles around her, and then explodes. The force of the spell picks her up and throws her against the wall again, destroying yet another stone figure extending from the wall.

Stunned Dak'tari slides down the wall, her leg catching upon the outstretched arm of some poor boil-covered elf girl, suffering from some sort of gruesome malaise. Hanging upside-down Dak'tari, her chest feeling as if it has been struck by a sledgehammer, knows that multiple ribs have been broken. Feigning unconsciousness she waits for Tha'gal to approach and finish her off. Hanging there she listens, judging the distance as his footsteps clack against the floor coming her way. Estimating that he is where she needs him to be she slips from the outstretched arm, holding her in place, and hits the floor. Blue-green flashes of pain dance in front of her eyes, as the impact with the floor jars her ribs. Ignoring the pain she rolls to her feet and flings the black blade, still clutched within her hand, up into the air. Arcing off into the heights, a sharp twang reverberates throughout the chamber as the blade servers the thick black iron chains holding the brazier suspended in the air, above the spot where Tha'gal now stands. Dak'tari diving away, gasping for air as her broken ribs press against her lungs.

The brazier, filled with the eerie purplish flame, tumbles from where it was hanging and smashes into the floor with an earth-shattering crash; cracking the stone flooring and crushing the high priest of Gauntlar beneath it. A howl of outrage and disbelief fills the room from where Tha'gal had stood. Followed by an explosion of purplish light, as the flame is extinguished, leaving Dak'tari momentarily blinded.

Regaining her eyesight, she goes to the spot where the fallen brazier slowly rocks back and forth; before finally coming to a rest on top of a pile of fine white power, which is all that remains of the lich. Running her fingers through the powder, her index finger catches upon the thin silver chain with the artifact, which she has come for, dangling from it. Grasping it, she tucks it into a pouch on her side just as the door flies open allowing the eight, red-armored guards from below to rush in.

Spotting her blade, once again a stiletto, lying on the floor about ten feet from her, she dashes towards it. Grasping it within her hand, it transforms into the katana which she had tried so hard to access before. Spinning to face two of the outraged guards, she brings the ebony blade around separating one's head from the rest of his body. Passing through his neck as if it didn't even exist, the blade continues its swing, cleaving a gaping gash through the armor and chest of the guard beside him.

As their blood flows across the cracked floor, she does a backflip landing on the gently rocking brazier. Balancing herself, she transforms her blade into a staff with two vicious-looking blades on both ends. Rushing Dak'tari, four of the guards are halted by either the separation of their heads from their necks or torso from the waist, as she brings the bladed staff down in a whirling circle around her body. Leaping off the huge caldron and over the fallen guards, she flips through the air, landing between the two remaining guards. Shoving one blade through the stomach of the guard behind her, she yanks it out and thrusts the opposite blade through the shoulder blades of the guard in front of her. Placing her foot on the guard she removes the blade from his back, as she does so it reverts into the stiletto, which she then places back in its place on her side.

Returning to the throne she searches for the secret compartment which she is sure must be there. After a few seconds, she finds, a small trap drawer located at the bottom of the throne. Disarming the trap she opens the drawer, a smile crosses her face as she removes a thumb-sized glowing diamond, which contains the soul of the lich. Placing it inside another pouch, she re-dons the guise of Ekthar and exits the wrecked chambers of the high priest.

Coming down the spiraling staircase, she passes numerous guards and priests running around frantically trying to figure out what has happened. Bellowing orders, from the throat of Ekthar, Dak'tari orders them to search for the human female who destroyed their high priest.

Passing through the pitch blackness of 'The Passageway to Death', she changes into the guise of an old crone which she had passed in the stairway.

Exiting the temple she passes the two guards standing outside, blocking entry to all and searching the crowd for a young human female. Allowing the old crone to exit, she heads down the steps in a limping shuffle and makes her way to the street. Passing a mass of people and creatures, trying to find out what is going on, she slowly hobbles towards the main gates and out of Passail.

Once out of sight of the city walls, she enters the oppressive darkness of the woods surrounding the city. Reaching into a pouch she removes a small scroll. Breaking the wax seal she recites the archaic words written upon the parchment. As she finishes the words the scroll disappears in a puff of smoke and ash, and Dak'tari finds herself standing in front of the ancient head of The Scarlet Brotherhood, seated upon his skull-strewn throne.

"It is done?" He asks, his yellow eyes burning into Dak'tari's red-flecked ones.

"It is done." She answers with a touch of self-pride. She reaches inside the pouches, extending her hands forward she hands over the Fingerbone of Gauntlar and the softly pulsating soul stone of Tha'gal.

Chapter III

TOWARDS THE WASTELANDS

I

Dak'tari followed the old man back into the weapons room. Entering the room the old man goes over to one of the iron cauldrons filled with the burning coals. Spitting into the palm of his right hand, he mumbles a few words and pulling back his sleeve, and thrusts his arm deep into the glowing coals. As his yellowed nail touches the bottom, he etches a symbol upon its blistering inner surface. After removing his arm the caldron begins to slide to the side, revealing a spiral staircase descending into inky blackness.

At the bottom of the staircase, Dak'tari finds herself in a thirty-foot diameter, circular room. Covering the walls, ceiling and floor are red runes of arcane power. Set in the center of the room stands a pedestal, made from what seems to be obsidian. Laying on the floor in a circle, around the pedestal, are eight mages with their heads towards the pedestal and feet pointing towards the eight points of the compass. At first, Dak'tari thinks they are dead. Then she notices the shallow, almost imperceptible, rising and falling of their chest, which shows they are alive and breathing.

"Drugged." Says the old man, noticing Dak'tari's questioning look." But not for long," he adds with a soft chuckle.

Stepping over the drugged mages, the old man leads Dak'tari to the black pedestal. Removing the Fingerbone of Gauntlar from his robes, he places it atop the obsidian stone. "You know what to do." It was not a question, more of a reaffirmation of the instructions he had given her upstairs.

"Yes." Her breathing became shallow with the excitement of anticipation.

Returning to the stairs the old man closes the door, sealing the gap in the rune-covered room, leaving Dak'tari alone with the eight mages.

Kneeling next to the mage, whose feet point towards the north, she removes her stiletto from its place at her side. Raising her blade above her head, she grasps it with both hands, the shimmering tip pointing towards the ceiling. Closing her eyes she whispers, "I'm ready my beloved."

With that the voice of her dark lord enters her mind, transforming her into a conduit for his dark will. She starts to chant, what the words are and what they mean she has no idea. But just as quickly as they come to her mind they exit her mouth in her voice. Thus beginning the spell that will transport her to the realm of the dead.

As the first words are spoken, she plunges her blade into the chest of the mage before her. Reaching down, still chanting, she reaches into the bloody gash and rips out the still-beating heart. Clutching the pulmonary organ in her hand she rises from the side of the corpse and walks over to where the finger bone lies. Extending her hand over the alter, she begins to squeeze the life juices from the still-beating heart. As the blood flows between her fingers it splatters upon the artifact. With the first drop, the runes in the room flare, come to life, and faintly start to pulsate. With each drop they grow stronger, absorbing the life force as the heart is slowly drained of it. Squeezing until the lumpy mass is completely drained she places the heart, which now resembles a large prune, on the north side of the alter.

Turning from the alter, the whole time continuing the chant, she moves to kneel beside the mage whose feet are pointing towards the northwest. Repeating the process she places his shriven heart on the northwest corner of the alter. She continues this until all the mages lay ripped open and empty. As each heart is drained the runes grow brighter and stronger in their pulsating intensity.

After setting the last heart upon the alter, Dak'tari slams the hilt of her stiletto down upon the blood-drenched fingerbone uttering the final words to the spell. The runes erupt and explode with the violent intensity of an atom split asunder. The force of the explosion is sucked into a vortex, which has formed above the pedestal. Dak'tari screams in tormented agony as she is ripped and torn apart molecule by molecule and sucked into the whirling vortex, along with the released energy of the spell.

Dak'tari awakes to the excruciating sensation that every muscle in her body has been savagely ripped apart and reattached by some sadistic physician. Laying face up she opens her eyes to find herself staring upon a gray, storm-filled sky. Sitting up, she gazes upon a blasted and bleak landscape, confused; she is not sure what has happened to her or where she is. Then as the ringing starts to fade from her ears, she hears the faint sound of tormented souls pleading and begging for absolution that will never come.

Then a sound, a sound which has never been heard upon this horrid landscape rings out. The sweet musical sound of a girl laughing in ecstasy.

"I've made it!" Dak'tari laughs. "I've made it, I'm in the realm of death!"

II

Setting out from Stalora, the group of humans, dwarves and elves travel down the Stalora branch of the Rea-lora Commerce Way, towards the fork at the Xaxtor Waterway and Stalora river. Towards nightfall, the group calls a halt at The Wandering Elf tavern, located about forty miles outside of Stalora. The tavern designed for the comfort of humans, elves and dwarves traveling the road, was rich in the comforts of all three races. Tables of wood and stone were neatly spaced around the room, while plants and flowers decorated the walls and corners.

Vesalin, coming down the stairs after washing and bathing, finds Deramar sitting alone by the crackling fire and sipping on a glass of mulled wine.

"May I join you?" She asks, coming up to the lone human.

"Yes, please." He answers, rising from his chair, indicating the empty seat next to him. "So, what finds you up and about at this time of the night."

"I couldn't sleep. I thought perhaps a glass of the inns' famous wine might help me fall asleep. How about yourself, why are you not sleeping?"

Calling over the waitress, Deramar orders Vesalin a glass of the same heated spiced wine that he is drinking. As the waitress leaves, after placing his order on the table, he answers her. "Ahh, well sometimes the past comes back to haunt me. I haven't had a chance to dwell on it too much lately, but this place got me to start thinking about my wife. We use to sit around the fireplace, telling stories about our day and sipping mulled wine while the children slept." He falls silent, a lost and longing pain filling his eyes, as he takes another sip of his wine.

"Where is she?" The elf asks innocently.

"Dead. Along with the children." He mutters.

"I'm sorry," Vesalin replies, flushing with embarrassment. "I didn't know."

"It's alright. It was a long time ago." He flashes a weak smile at the elf, before ordering them another round of wine.

After a moment of awkward silence, Deramar starts asking her about herself and her life in Stalora. Instantly her deep, rich amethyst eyes light up, casting her in a beautiful radiance, as she recalls the happy and joyous moments of her life. It doesn't take long before they are both laughing and smiling together, enjoying each other's company and the brief soft touches of their hands making contact on numerous occasions.

Finally, after a few hours of enjoying each other 's company, Vesalin arises. "Well, I guess I should be going to bed. It's getting fairly late. It was a pleasure," she adds with a smile.

"My lady the pleasure was all mine," Deramar says with a bow over her hand which he has taken. "Goodnight." Then gently touching her hand with his lips, he lets her slip away back upstairs to her room.

As the party rides throughout the next day, it is missed by no one that Deramar and Vesalin ride next to each other talking and laughing along the whole ride. This is especially true of Mizzan, who turns frequently to scowl back at the two. Disapproving strongly of his sister, a royal princess, associating so openly and friendly with not only a commoner but a human as well.

By late afternoon of the next day, they reach the fork of the two rivers. Relief and joy fill the dwarves, as they spot a contingent of their kinsmen waiting for them on the docks to the dwarven riverboat, which will take them to the gates of Xaxtor.

Seeing the party riding up, a group of bare-chested dwarves breaks from the rest of the waiting dwarves. Rushing up the gangplank they commence to get the riverboat ready for departure. The remaining dwarves, dressed in the gleaming steel and golden armor which proclaims them members of The Golden Vein, snap to attention along the gangplank.

The party, led by Principal Citizen Steelstone, comes to halt before the guards. As Kash dismounts from his long-haired hill pony, the lead guard steps forward and seizes the reins. The hill pony is a beautiful, rich auburn-colored creature with the stout muscle tone and strength of the dwarves themselves. Raised by the dwarves for their use, they find these short, sure-footed animals are much more to their taste, who have a distinct distrust of their larger cousins. They of course would never admit that they were terrified of the full-sized creatures.

"Any word from Xaxtor?" Kash asks of the guard holding the reins.

"No Principal Citizen. Wees' gotten no word since youse departed."

"Good. Prepare to sail for home as soon as the animals are stowed below." Kash orders, as he strides up the gangplank onto the deck of the riverboat.

Following him the rest of their party board the riverboat, leading their horses and ponies below deck and stowing them away. After making sure his horse has been taken care of, Deramar returns to the upper deck to explore the dwarven riverboat.

Though they have an intense fear of the high seas, and the ships that sail upon them, the dwarven riverboats are the envy of all Tamara. Forty feet long and twenty feet wide with a flat bottom, these vessels are made up completely of black wrought iron. Sitting ten feet back from the bow is the ten-foot-wide and fifteen-foot long pilothouse, which controls the steering for the double keel mounted beneath the boat. At the stern is the five-foot-long and twenty-foot wide furnace housing, with two exhaust stacks extending from the roof bellowing steam. Two bare-chested dwarven sailors shovel coal into a furnace supplying heat for the boiler and powering the engine, mounted below deck. The paddlewheel attached to the rear of the vessel is fifteen feet in diameter and twenty-five feet long, with wooden slats that churn up the river and propel the ship forward. Two iron beams, mounted to the axles and hubs extending from both sides of the paddlewheel and gear house, hold the wheel in place, while chains looped around sprockets, also mounted to the axles, transfer the energy from the engine to the paddlewheel.

Deramar standing on deck, hands resting on the rails, watches the bank slip pass and listens to the soothing whush, whush, whush of the paddlewheel cutting through the water. The sun just starting to slip beyond the horizon turns the water a brilliant purple, crowned with a fiery orange that dances upon the delicately lapping waves. The soft tread of footsteps upon the metal deck tears him from his tranquil contemplation to see Vesalin approaching him. Stopping to stand beside him, the gentle breeze catches the fine tresses of her golden hair causing it to flutter around her face like fine golden strings of spiderwebs. Reaching up she gathers it together with a slim finger and tucks it behind a delicately pointed ear.

"Beautiful, is it not?" She says gazing upon the water, setting a hand on the railing next to his.

"Yes, it is." He replies, clasping her eyes within his smiling gaze. Reaching up he brushes back a lock of hair that had again come loose from behind her ear.

Her smooth hand rises from the rail to gently wrap around his rough one, which is lovingly caressing her cheek with a callused thumb.

"I was talking about the water." She replies, smiling sweetly as a blush starts to infuse her soft, alabaster cheek.

"So was 1?" He smiles back, raising his other hand to take her upturned face and pull it to his.

Suddenly the magical moment is shattered by the indignant, enraged voice of Mizzan coming from behind them. "What in the hell do you think you are doing human?" Turning they face the furious visage of Vesalin's brother, standing before them like the embodiment of disapproval itself.

"What is it to you elf?" Deramar hisses through clenched teeth, stepping forward to place himself in the elf's face. His body tensing, to that of an overly-wound spring ready to snap Mizzan at the slightest indication that the elf wishes to brawl. He was getting quite tired of the elf's dirty looks since he and Vesalin had started to get acquainted.

Quickly stepping between the two fuming warriors, Vesalin places a restraining hand on Deramar's shoulder. "Please Deramar, could you excuse us for a moment?"

Taking a half-step backward, his eyes still locked with Mizzan's, he takes Vesalin's hand from his shoulder and bowing his head presses it to his lips. Mizzan trembles in impotent rage as Deramar's eyes twinkle with impish glee. Dropping her hand from his lips he rises. "Till we meet again, my lady." Then turning he strides confidently past the pilothouse and onto the bow of the boat.

As Deramar passes out of sight Vesalin whirls on her brother. "What was that about?" The fury in her voice matched the rising red tinge creeping up her neck.

"What were you doing with that *human*?" Mizzan spits out the last word as if it was a piece of rancid meat.

Mizzan is taken off guard by the fury that flashes within the almond-shaped eyes of the Vesalin. "What I do, and with whom I do it with is none of your concern!" Reaching up she pokes a finely manicured and painted nail into his chainmail-covered chest. "Do you understand me?" Waving her hand in dismissal, she turns her back on the infuriated elf and heads towards the bow and Deramar. "Now go away, and don't meddle in my affairs again!"

"I will not allow you to taint our noble blood, sister!" He calls at her back before turning himself and heading below deck.

As gentle as the fragrance that she daubs on her neck and heaving bosom, Vesalin places a hand on Derarnar's shoulder. Clasping her hand, he turns from the darkness and slips his other arm around her slim waist, and pulls her to him. Engulfing her within the warmth of his body, he whispers into her ear. "Are you sure you want to do this?"

Her voice coming through the deep sighs of anticipation, enhances the tiny trembles coursing through her body. "No I'm not sure, but I want to anyway."

Sliding his hand up her side, he cups the back of her neck and pulls her face towards his. The taste is like the sweetest of elven wines as he drinks in her lips. Feeling the stirring of his manhood, she presses her body even tighter against his, grinding her pelvis against his crotch.

As their passions begin to engulf them, the heavy tread of booted feet heading towards the bow causes them to pull apart. From around the corner of the pilot, house steps one of the dwarven sailors carrying a torch. Stopping at the rail he reaches out and begins to ignite the lamps that light up the deck of the riverboat in the darkness.

With a sigh and a little more than a tinge of regret in her eyes, Vesalin reaches up stokes Deramar's cheek, and walks away heading below deck to her quarters.

Deramar leans against the rail watching the dwarf make his rounds from lantern to lantern, lighting each one in turn. While on the other side of the pilothouse, a figure cloaked in darkness, silently slips away, his almond-shaped eyes burning with a fiery hatred.

III

As the morning sun rises, its golden rays show not only the new day but also The Grand Watershed Gate of Xaxtor. Pouring down from the top of the mountain is a massive waterfall, flowing down like a sheet of sparkling diamonds. The great sheet is split into two equal parts by a gargantuan double-bladed axe, carved from the stone wall and extending into the center of the falls. The two sparkling ribbons then flow down into the top of two equally huge ale steins, also carved from the rock face. Through a large channel cut into the back of the steins, the two rivers then flow back into the mountain to be used by the dwarves. After the water has served its purpose, it then flows back into The Xaxtor Waterway through two huge horizontal slits cut into the side of the mountain and funneled back into the river by two river-sized aqueducts. As the water pours back into the river, it causes such a tidal pool of swirling, thrashing water that nothing other than the dwarf's steam-powered boats could pass it.

The gate itself sits back nearly one hundred yards from the face of the mountain. The large cavern is filled with a network of docks and piers, where dwarven dock-workers are busy loading and unloading supplies from more of the ironclad riverboats.

Docking at a pier located towards the rear of the cavern, the group disembarks and makes their way towards the fifty-foot tall set of double doors standing open. Made from the finest dwarven steel, they are engraved with the glorious exploits of the dwarves for the last thousand years. Set in the center of the doors is the face of Xax, the dwarven god, made from gold, silver, and copper. Encircling the faces is a wide band of precious gems. Passing through the doors they are led into the halls of Xaxtor. To either side of them is another set of aqueducts that catches the water from the steins and disappears off into the distance.

At the end of the hall, they come to a massive network of steel rails branching off in a myriad of directions, like a huge steel spiderweb. Steam-powered vehicles rumble back and forth along the rails like metallic behemoths, belching and bellowing steam as they chug past, carrying goods and passengers. The tumultuous noise they create is a tooth-aching, ear-shattering cacophony of releasing gases and squealing steel, that the humans find torturous and the elves excruciatingly unbearable. With their fingers shoved into their ears, they make their way to a waiting car, under the jovial laughter of the dwarves.

Once inside and the door slides close, the clamor from outside diminishes to almost nothing. Seated in the iron benches they are jerked forward then thrust back as the car begins to roll forward, taking them down one of the many tunnels.

Dyrgen, after wiggling his little finger in his ear, as if trying to remove a ball of cotton wedged down there, turns to Kash. "Well, I must say Principal Citizen. I had heard stories of your fabulous transit system, but only half-believed them and never thought I would get to ride on it. Now that I have seen it with my own eyes the stories didn't do it justice." A broad smile of pleasure and wonder spread across his red-bearded face. "Very impressive, very impressive indeed."

"Why thank youse, captain." Kash's short, stocky body swells with the pride of his peoples' ingenuity. "This is just one of the many devices we'es is proud of."

"Monstrous is what I think it is!" Mizzan spits, not even attempting to hide his contempt for the amazing device.

Elstar whirls on Mizzan. "You will hold a civil tongue as long as we are guests here! Do you understand?" Then the irritation slips away to be replaced by concern. "What is troubling you Mizzan? You have been short-tempered since we left Stalora."

"Nothing." He replies, not very convincingly. "Perhaps I just miss the forest. All this stone and metal makes me uncomfortable." But the darting, scathing glance cast under hooded eyes, towards

Vesalin and Deramar is missed by none, who are all aware of the growing relationship between the two.

Sighing, Elstar clasps Mizzan 's shoulder. "I miss home to my prince. But we have a long journey before us and the longing for home will only grow stronger the farther we get from it." Squeezing the angry elf's shoulder his eyes bore into his. "We were sent by your father to determine what is going on in The Northern Waste. That is our only concern. Not our feelings and not what others may do. Unless it affects our mission." The minute emphasis on this last statement was meant for Vesalin and Deramar. "All that matters is determining if there is a threat brewing up there and returning back safely. O.K?"

A slight nod of Mizzan's head and an easing of the tension in his body is the only response that Elstar receives.

Dropping his hand, Elstar casts an apologetic grin towards Kash. "Now Principal Citizen, what is your plan?"

"First," he replies, tearing his fierce eyes from Mizzan to focus them upon Elstar. "Youse will be taken to quarters where youse can rest. Tomorrow we're will meet to discuss youse mission. We're will be arriving at youse station in about fifteen minutes. I's is going to see if any news from the north has come since I's been gone. But I's leave youse in good company." Waving a thick arm towards Grundel and Crundor. "Vorrax will be coming with me'es for now." His round, gray-bearded face splits into a grin as he turns towards Dyrgen. "But don't youse worry. I's will let him's rejoin youse latter, so youse can sample a real tavern." He pauses, looking sternly at the big knight. "All I's ask is that youse don't kill anybodies, or each other's." The belting laughter of the dwarves starts the railcar to rocking. While the thumping wallop Kash slaps upon Dyrgen's back, which would have sent a smaller man careening across the car, causes the knight to burst into whooping mirth.

"I make no promises Principal Citizen," he replies through his laughter. "But I'll do my best." The humor of the moment alleviates the tension which had been building within the car.

A few minutes later the railcar comes to a grinding, squeaking, shambling halt. The steam released from the boiler greets those disembarking like an angry dragon, as they step out onto the platform. Standing on the platform waiting for them were six, what the dwarves would consider beautiful, dwarven females. Their short, evenly trimmed beards were combed and studded with glistening gems. Each one of the dwarven women, taking charge of their assigned human or elf, leads them to their respective quarters, while the two male dwarves make their way to their chambers.

"Hello, sir'rah. My's name is Bethal, and I's will be taking care of youse while youse stay with us'es. If youse please, follow me'es." Says one of the female dwarves to Deramar. Following her, she leads him down a hall to a thick stone door. "This is youse room." She opens the door to a large spacious chamber. The spartan stone room is complete without fanfare, as is the dwarven style. No tapestries cover the walls and no rugs blanket the polished stone floor. The table, two chairs, and bed frame are all made from a dark gray stone. The only cloth in the whole room was the mattress and blankets, provided for the guests; since the dwarves prefer to feel stone or metal beneath them at all times, even while sleeping.

"Well sir'rah, I's will return shortly with some food and drink." Indicating a button next to the door, Bethal continues before leaving. "If youse need anything, just push this and I's be right here." Flashing a bright smile through her light beard, she bows, exits the room, and closes the door behind her.

Having had turned down Dyrgen's offer earlier to go out and cause some sort of ruckus in one of the many dwarven taverns, Deramar lays upon his bed after exploring the wonders of the dwarven city. His belly full from the meal brought to him by Bethal, he allows his eyes to drift shut from the effects of the strong, dark-brown dwarven ale.

A gentle rapping upon his door brings him instantly awake and to his feet. Opening the thick stone door, Deramar's eyes widened in pleasant surprise at the sight of Vesalin standing there in a sheer, turquoise-blue, robe. Stepping aside, he allows the scantily clad elf into his room. As Deramar closes the door, Vesalin allows the near see-through cloth to slip from her shoulders and puddle around her feet. Standing within the folds of the cloth, like an angel emerging from a clear mountain pool, she trembles with hesitant anticipation. Then suddenly she flings herself into Deramar's waiting arms and lips. Lifting her, he softly places her atop the mound of blankets on the bed, covering her lips, neck, and eyes with deep, passionate kisses. Rising from her he slips out of his clothes and rejoins her waiting embrace on top of the woolen blankets, allowing their passions to consume them.

Hours later she arises, both their bodies and blankets soaked from their lovemaking, and re-dons her robe. Kissing him one last time, she slips from the room and back into the hall. Drifting back towards sleep, breathing in the lingering aroma of her scent, he realizes that not a word had been spoken between them. Smiling with satisfaction, he falls into the deep sleep of the sated.

✶✶✶✶✶

A steady persistent knocking upon the door causes Deramar to arise from the soft warm comfort of his bed. Opening the door he finds Bethal holding a steaming platter of beef, bread, and ale.

"Morning sir'rah." She says, greeting him with a warm smile on her fuzzy face. "I's have youse breakfast."

Walking to the table she sets the food down. "Principal Citizen Steelstone expects youse presence in an hour." Turning from the table she makes for the door. "I's be back to get youse then." Bowing she leaves the room.

At the appointed hour Deramar finds himself in a beautifullycarved chamber, the four walls sculpted with depictions of dwarves doing what they love to do the most. To the north, it shows dwarves mining out great caverns of enormous beauty. To the west are diminutive artisans sculpting exquisite statues, so life-like they seem on the verge of stepping from the wall and taking their place within the room. The south wall is covered in dwarven ironworkers and craftsmen hammering and molding great weapons of power, the armor of incredible strength, and jewelry of the finest quality. While to the east are represented as the machinist and technicians, creating the wondrous machines that the dwarves are so proud of.

Set in the center of the room is a massive stone table made from a deep, almost black, green stone with veins of gold running throughout it. Laying on the table, which the group is gathered around, lays a map of Xaxtor and The Northern Waste.

"Here is where we'es believe this reportedly 'dark force' is located." Reaching out his arm Kash taps a spot due north of Xax Mountain. "We'es believe there is a portal or void forming in this area. The scout that made it back here rambled on about 'hole in the world, hole in the world, the dark force has come, the dark force has come.' that was all we'es could get out of him before he died. We'se need youse to find out if it is a portal. And if so, where does it go, whose made it, and for what purpose."

Pausing he reaches over, lifts a gold and jewel-encrusted stein of ale, and drains it empty. Cussing, he flings the stein against the wall, chipping the image of a riverboat on the east wall and denting the golden stein with a resounding clang. "Damn!" The ale froth flying from his beard and mustache in his fury. Then as quickly as it came upon him, his anger is gone leaving him drained and looking like an ancient specter of his normally vital self.

"I's sorry," he barely whispers. "I's just wish I's had more information for youse. I's received new reports that orcs'es, trolls'es, and other foul creatures seem to be moving in that direction. More than that we'es know nothing. Go gather youse gear. Youse will be taken to the north gate. Good luck; I's fear that the fate of all Tamora is in youse hands, not just my's kingdom. Now please leave me'es." With a near imperceptible wave of his hand, he adjourns the meeting.

Sometime later the nine companions find themselves in one of the ironclad railcars making for the north gate. Not since arriving in Xaxtor had Deramar and Vesalin spoken a word to each other, their words no longer seemed nearly as important to them as their feelings for each other. Sitting Next to Deramar, Vesalin reaches over picks up his hand, sets it in her lap, and squeezes it as if afraid he might slip through her fingers. Then lifting it from her lap, she places it against her pounding heart.

Suddenly all hell breaks loose on the car as Mizzan, no longer able to contain his outrage, leaps to his feet and springs at Deramar with a dagger in his hand. Before anybody has a chance to react Deramar has Mizzan disarmed, thrust up against the vibrating wall of the railcar and Mizzan's dagger pricking the skin between the elf's ribs, allowing a single drop of blood to drip down its gleaming edge. The speed of the reversal stuns Mizzan, along with the rest of the group, and the cold, soulless eyes of a professional killer, containing no compassion, caring or remorse leaves Mizzan sure that he is about to die.

A scream rips apart the stunned silence within the metal cabin. "No! Please don't." Begs Vesalin placed a quivering, restraining hand on Deramar's shoulder. She breathes a sigh of relief as she feels the tension ease from Deramar's shoulder.

"It is only because of your sister and the love I have for her that you live," the human hisses icily. The hand holding the dagger withdraws from the elf's side, while the hand clutched around his throat releases. Mizzan gasps as airflow back into his lungs and blood rushes back into his bluish-purple face. Then like a striking snake, a fist slams into the elf's jaw-dropping him into unconsciousness.

Turning from the sprawled elf, Deramar faces the stunned shocked gazes of the party. Speaking to Elstar he says flatly. "I will not go on if I have to be concerned about getting a knife or arrow in my back. So either you send him back home or I go."

Elstar starts to bristle at the ultimatum, then slowly exhales and glances at each member of the group. One by one they each nod their heads in quiet assent. Finally, he turns to Vesalin.

"He's right." She says through her soft sobs. "We don't know what we are getting into. We have to be able to trust each other with our lives. Mizzan's prejudices have blinded him to what is important." Covering her face with her hands she starts to cry uncontrollably. "It's all my fault. It's all my fault."

Going to her, Deramar wraps his arms around her. She tries to pull away but he only holds her tighter. Finally consenting to his embrace she melts within his arms, crying on his chest.

Kissing her on top of the head he whispers soothingly. "We can't help what we feel, my love." Taking her under the chin he lifts her tear-streaked face upwards. "I love you, my princess." He smiles, kissing a red swollen eye. "I love you," he repeats, kissing her other eye.

The jerking halt of the railcar brings Mizzan back to consciousness. Rising from the floor, rubbing his chin he stands silently, eyes downcast in shame as the humans and dwarves file past, leaving him alone with his brethren.

Veselin goes to her brother, taking him by the hands. Mizzan jerks away as if burned "Get away from me Slut!"

For a moment her lips start to quiver as tears begin to flow from her eyes. Then angrily she pushes back the tears and slaps him across the face, "Deramar was right about you." Squaring her shoulders she turns and exits the car.

Elstar glares with visible disgust at his prince.

"Your journeys end here, my prince," he states coldly. "Go home. The company will allow you to travel no farther."

"You can't keep me from going!" Mizzan flares.

"Yes, I can!" Elstar replies just as hotly. "You might be my prince. But your father placed you under my command. Your attitude threatens the success of this mission, So therefore you will go no farther with us."

"How can you condone the mating of that human," he spits the word as if it were a curse, "with one of the royal line!"

"Enough!" Elstar commands. "Go home or stay here. I no longer care. Either way, you will not be continuing with us. "Spinning, Elstar leaves Mizzan glaring at his back as he exits the car to join the waiting party.

The door to the car slides shut, taking Mizzan back in the direction from which they just came; and the remaining members of the group standing on the platform, readying their gear for the long, cold journey ahead.

Chapter IV

INTO THE WASTELANDS

I

The dust-ridden, apocalyptic landscape, which is the realm of Gauntlar, resembled a long lost, haunted, and forgotten graveyard. Blasted, rotted, dead trees dot the landscape like skeletal hands clawing from the reddish-brown earth, reaching for the storm-swept sky. Screaming and howling like a banshee, the wind beats upon the eardrums as if it was the drums of hell summoning forth all the damned souls of the abyss; while lurking deep within its depths comes the ever-present moaning and wails of despair of those banished to this horrid land.

Clouds of dust and sand, whipped up by the screaming torrent, rips, and claws at the flesh and clothing as if hungry to taste the gleaming white bones hidden beneath the soft, juicy casing.

Tumbleweeds and brush bounce, roll, and are caught within the grips of the whirling dervishes to be flung into the air. Sent spinning through the hazy atmosphere, they fly hundreds of yards before falling back onto the plains to begin their jaunty dance again.

As Dak'tari gazes upon the retched landscape a strange, almost peculiar feeling comes over her. At first, she can't quite put her finger on the problem, then as time slips by she begins to realize what it is. Clawing at her throat, she struggles and gasps for the air which refuses to enter her lungs. Even though the land and sky are thrashed by a raging gale, the air itself contains no life-giving oxygen, for the dead do not need breath. Her eyes begin to bulge, as her face begins to turn a sickly shade of blue from oxygen deprivation. Falling to the ground in an ever-increasing, blackening haze, she kicks, thrashes, bucks, and continues to claw at her throat as she struggles to fill her lungs to no avail. Then just as she starts to slip into the unconsciousness that foreshadows the oncoming of death, a strange, peculiar, tingling sensation courses through her body. Feeling as if all her blood has started to boil, threatening the engulf her in flames from the inside out, she lets out a horrific scream of unending agony. Then sucks in a lung full of the choking, gagging dust that swirls around her. Choking and panting she vomits the dust she has just inhaled back upon the land. Hovering over the pile of dusty puke, on quivery hands and knees, she slowly and steadily begins to breathe in the oxygen-free air. At first, confused as to what has just occurred, it finally dawns on her air-starved brain as the words of Cantanis return to her. 'You will start to gain the gifts of demon-kind as time goes on and the need arises.' Smiling feebly, still weak and trembling, she gives thanks, not to her mother (who means nothing to her), but to her mother's blood which courses through her veins.

Rising to her feet she reforms her suit, of dark-elf skin, into an ochre-colored cloak and mask, which she pulls over her nose and mouth to block the dust.

Rapped within the folds of her cloak, which blends perfectly with the landscape, she shields her eyes with a hand and scans the far horizon. Off in the distance, she spots a mountain range, resembling the broken, shattered teeth of a skull. Shrugging her shoulders, she mutters, "Well, it is as good a direction as any." So, not seeing any other landmarks in any other direction, she makes sure her blade is still in its place at her side and heads off towards the mountains.

Dak'tari continues walking towards the mountains, never seeing any sign of the spirits that are supposed to inhabit this plane;

other than the constant moaning floating upon the wind, which she begins to fear is a trick of the wind itself. Slowly an uncontrollable fear of dread starts to eat at her insides, like a ravenous tapeworm, as she starts to believe that something must have gone wrong with her spell and that she was not on the plane of Gauntlar.

Finally, after hours, days, weeks, she has no idea which in the never-changing twilight aspect of the oppressive landscape, Dak'tari trudges on towards the mountains. Each plodding step carries with it the ever-growing need for water within her dust-filled throat, growing weaker and weaker she stumbles along hoping desperately for at least a rancid pool of fluid to appear before her. Her eyesight goes hazy, her mind grows frantic as her body screams for at least the tiniest drop of the precious fluid. Finally, as she sways before the pass between two of the shattered peaks, she stumbles, wobbles, and then collapses in a heap of exhaustion and cloying thirst. Pulling herself to her trembling hands and knees, she claws forward a few more feet before her arms give out, dropping her face back into the dust.

Delirious from thirst and anguish, she flutters in and out of consciousness. Consciousness brings the burning, heat scorching rawness which is her throat. Unconsciousness brings with it the tranquil refreshment from a plunge into a clear mountain stream. Consciousness, the dust-filled agonizing delirium of water deprivation. Unconsciousness brings a tingling, electrical sensation coursing through her body from the tip of her toes to the ends of her hair. Steadily the sensation builds, growing ever stronger to become a crescendo of magical power as it is discharged from her body. As the energy is released, it leaves her confused as to what has just happened to her. The surprise and wonder force her to raise her face from the powdery dust.

Thick with the crusty mud of tears, she pries her bleary eyes open with a tearing wrench. Gazing in shock and disbelief as her eyes focus on the large pitcher of cooling water, which had appeared in her mind's eye and now sits before her. The sight is like a shot of adrenaline to her body. Strength flows into her quaking arms, allowing her to claw herself forward to the waiting pitcher. Clutching for it hesitantly, expecting at any moment that it shall suddenly vanish back in the air from which it apparently came. Trembling, hoping, praying to her dark lord that this is not a mirage or trick of her feverish mind, her hand closes around the cool handle of the waiting jug of water. Grabbing it with one hand, she reaches up with the other and rips the mask from her face, and pours the cool water down her parched throat. With each gulp she feels life flow back into her, invigorating her and restoring her strength. When her thirst is sated, she pours the remainder over her face and head, only then wondering where it had come from.

Sitting back, resting against the foot of the mountains, she remembers the flashes between consciousness and unconsciousness; along with the building and release of magical energy.

"But how?" She wonders aloud. Then the words of Cantanis come to her again concerning her heritage.

"Can it be, can it be?" Not sure if she had performed this small feat of magic, she decides to test it. Closing her eyes, she again pictures a jug of cold water. Again the tingling sensation arises in her to be discharged on the ground before her. Opening her eyes, she laughs in triumph at the sight of the water before her. Grabbing it, she over-turns it above her head and lets it run down her head and over her body. Ignoring the mud that clings to her face, from the combination of dust and water, her chest swells in elation and pride at the newfound gift of her mother's blood.

Though small in comparison to the possibility of lightning bolts and fireballs, this came when most needed. Whereas a fireball would have been as useful as the boulder she was laying against. This small, insignificant, but useful cantrip had saved her life, but more importantly, it allowed her to continue on her mission for her beloved. For that reason she knew, whereas no person, animal, or anything else other than her dark lord, that near insignificant spell would always possess a small portion of her dark heart.

Finally, as the excitement dwindles, she regains her composer. Rising she rubs the mud from her face, which does more to smear it than make it go away, and enters into the pass.

Continuing through the pass, the walls of the cliffs creep ever closer onto the winding trail threatening to close it off at some point. As the pass becomes narrower, the raging winds of the open plain are funneled down to become the howling, buffeting fury of a hurricane. Pounding her unmercifully, the gale knocks her from her feet and slams her into the rock face repeatedly. Regaining her feet she claws at the walls, struggling to remain on her feet, only to be knocked down and sent tumbling against the wall time after time.

Finding a protruding boulder she clings to the leeward side, like a spider, digging her fingers into the thin cracks that mar its surface. Raising her face towards the sky she curses the wind, the fury of the gale pales in comparison to the fury in her words, but yet they still fall on deaf ears as the gale refuses to abate in the slightest.

Her fingernails broken and bleeding, her arms and legs trembling and growing ever weaker from her journey to the mountains and losing the fight against the wind, she looks about in despair hoping to find some sort of refuse from the storm. Then she spots it, the small gaping maw of a cave entrance not twenty feet from her. Releasing her precarious hold upon the rock, she tumbles and rolls aiming desperately for the refuge of the cave. Tumbling past the entrance her hands leap out and snag the lip of the hole. With the last reserves of her strength, she ever so slowly pulls herself to the maw. Released from the clawing grip of the wind she collapses against the inside wall of the cave in exhaustion.

After a few minutes, she rises to her shaky feet and moves off warily into the inky black recesses of the cave. As the light from outside vanishes her hell-spawned eyes flash, allowing her the see clearly in the darkness. Continuing back, the floor beneath her feet begins to slope downwards, growing ever steeper with each step. The oppressive gloom of the cave presses in upon her, trying to block her descent farther into its depths as if it were a tangible creature with a life force and malignant will of its own. Like the crushing depths of the ocean squeezing down upon the hull of a submersible, the pressure of the thick, humid air becomes nearly unbearable. Each labored intake of air seems to be filled with fetid, cloying rottenness, that starts to make her feel lightheaded and nauseous. Feeling dizzy, she starts to consider turning back when her foot slips on a loose rock sending her tumbling head over heels down the slope. With a sudden halt, her head fills with the sharp, stinging sparks of pain as it connects with an up-thrusting tongue of rock. Then she slips into the blackness of unconsciousness, and she feels nothing.

II

For two long, cold, frigid days and nights the party moved through the frozen barren, snow-covered arctic wasteland of the north seeing nothing except ice, ice, and more ice. The dreary and depressing sun, a pale, pathetic shadow of its normally glorious self, remained obscured by the driving snow, gray clouds, and freezing, bonenumbing sleet. The overall oppressive atmosphere of the wasteland seemed to drain the morale from the party just as quickly as the cold drained the warmth from their bodies. Shambling on, heads down and thick fur cloaks pulled tight around them, they struggled through the bleak heartless landscape. The worst-hit seemed to be Vesalin who for those two days says nothing to no one, blaming herself for Mizzan's fall from the company's graces, and only eating when forced by Elstar. Several times Deramar had gone to her, trying to comfort her and soothe her pain, but each time he was rebuffed by a distant and vacant stare.

On the morning of the third day out of Xaxtor, the group finds themselves staring into the great yawning abyss of a chasm torn into the glacier, which they have been treading upon for the last day and a half. The far-side, over two hundred feet away, can barely be made out in the pale ghostly sunlight and falling snow. The party stares at the gaping maw, laughing before them, heads downcasted and huddled within their thick furs.

"What now?" Asks Grundel, stomping his feet to keep them warm.

"We'es follow the bloody ledge till we'es find a way across! What the hell do youse think?" Vorrax retorts, spitting towards the icy canyon. Instead of flying into the gulf, it snags onto the fluttering hair of his beard. Where it quickly turns into a tiny icicle, matching the ones already hanging there.

As the group prepares to continue their journey along the glaciers edge, a weak voice is heard coming from the back.

"Wait." Vesalin finally speaks, after her days of self-imposed silence. Stepping between the gathered group, she walks to the edge of the chasm. Removing a glove, she reaches down and gathers up a handful of snow. Rising back up, she begins chanting softly in a sing-song voice. As she continues with her spell, her voice grows steadily stronger and more commanding. Then in a flurry, she cast the snow before her and across the crevice. Spreading out before her, the snow flutters down, elongates, and crystallizes into a thick, solid ice bridge spanning the void. As she turns back towards the surprised party, they are overjoyed to see that for the first time in days, a thin, beautiful smile graces her elegant features as she begins to make her way across the bridge.

After the days of somber trudging, life once again seemed to infuse the party. The dwarves still grumbled about the ice and snow, though it is more the normal displeasure of being cold; than the harsh curses damning the frozen wasteland to the fiery forge of Xax. Darl, whose constant dour expression is as permanent a feature to his face as the snow is to this land, seemed more relaxed and at ease. He once even nearly approached a smile, as Dyrgen cracked a very crude joke, concerning a troll, an orc, a goblin, and a very uncomfortable (if not impossible) position for the goblin. But best of all was the squeak of embarrassed laughter that came from Vesalin, at the punch line, which set everyone to laugh. For the rest of the day, the party traveled in extremely high spirits, feeling renewed and invigorated by Vesalin's return from her melancholy solitude.

At nightfall the group sits huddled around each other for warmth, refusing to light a fire. Not only because it might be seen from a distance, but also due to the fact that there was nothing to burn. As they sit around talking and enjoying each other's company, they are suddenly interrupted by the piercing howls from a pack of wolves.

The maddening howls of the wolves on the hunt echo upon the chilling wind of the night. The darkness from the omnipresent clouds and snow, which obscures the light from the moon, cloaks and hides all within its black folds, hiding nearly completely anything within its chilling embrace; as ever nearer comes the fearsome howls, approaching at a speed that rivals the wind, straight towards them.

"Wolves'es." Crundor says menacingly, as his fingers tighten around the haft of his ax.

"Those are not wolves," informs Elstar. "They're worgs."

As suddenly as it started the howling comes to an abrupt end, leaving the darkness as quiet as a morgue at midnight.

Then like a meteor out of the night, a massive, black snarling mass of matted fur with gnashing teeth and tusks slams into the back of Grundel, smashing him to the ground and crushing his skull with one snap of its powerful jaws.

Crundor, seeing his fallen kinsmen flies into a berserker rage. Bellowing a warcry he charges the beast, swinging his axe around in a circle. Coming up from underneath the worg's head, the blade catches the creature in the neck sending the severed head spinning off into the darkness.

A pale blue glowing sphere appears above Vesalin, answering her chanting and casting the area around the surrounded party in gentle light, showing the menace that confronts them.

The body of a wolf and the head of a boar, these fearsome creatures are two hundred and fifty pounds of muscle and hatred. Covering their frames is thick, black matted fur, reeking of the rotting flesh and waste which makes the flooring of their dens. Two beady, malicious eyes, flashing red in the magical light, sit above the wrinkled, hairless snouts, which contain two six-inch long tusks protruding upwards and dripping saliva.

They pad around the group in a wary circle, eyeing them with wrathful, sadistic hatred. Then as one, they charge the party.

Two drop-in quick successions as Elstar pierces their tiny brains, with an arrow inserted through the eye of each of them. Vorrax and Crundor, insane with rage at the death of their fallen kinsman, hack three to pieces with the psychopathic abandon of a psychotic butcher. Darl, pinning one's head to the ground with his war-pick, slits its throat with a dagger, leaving it twitching in the snow while the blood flows from its jugular. Another worg bursts into flames, yowling in pain, from the spell cast by Vesalin. Flopping to the ground it twists and rolls about trying to put out its burning coat. Then collapsing it falls still, as a thick, inky black gagging smoke arises from off its charred body. Yet another drops, its neck broke from the shattering impact of Dyrgen's shield; which he quickly follows up with a thrust of his sword to its heart.

Deramar drops to his back beneath the leaping mass of teeth and claws, and slashes open a worg's belly as it passes over him, to fall in a tangle of guts and entrails. Allowing his momentum to carry him, he continues his back-roll and goes into a flip, landing on the back of the last worg which he impales through the skull with his sword, just feet from Vesalin who was its target.

Rising from the beast he has just slain, Deramar looks at Vesalin (making sure she is alright) and flashes her a bright grin of relief while wiping the blood from his face. Vesalin stares down in amazement at the creature lying before her feet, then rushes into Deramar's waiting arms and bestows a deep kiss of thanks and undying love upon his lips.

Pulling apart they look around to see Darl and Dyrgen both prying their weapons free from the carcasses of the beast they have slain. While Elstar retrieves his two arrows. Then their eyes fall on the two dwarves standing over the mangled body of their fallen friend.

Slowly the surviving members of the group make their way over to their fallen comrade. Standing solemn and silent they gaze down with growing grief upon the slain dwarf. The wind whistling across the frozen landscape, playing a lonely dirge of loss and death, is the only sound for long moments.

"We'es need to build a pyre for ours'es brother." Crundor finally says, the grief thick and palpable in his voice.

"We can't." Elstar replies, his voice full of heartfelt regret." A fire would be seen for miles. Besides, my friend, there is no wood, nothing with which we could build a pyre."

"We'es can't leave him's here, with these'es foul creatures'es." Vorrax proclaims, viciously kicking a worg he has just hacked to pieces. "He'es needs to be consumed by fire, so he'es can take his place at Xax's forge."

"Perhaps I can help, my dear friends," Vesalin says gently, kneeling down before the dwarves and taking their hands within hers. "Though it will not be a pyre, I can see that his body is consumed by heat. Would that satisfy Xax?"

"If the heat is hot enough to consume his'es bones, my lady," Vorrax answers, with a tinge of hope. "It should do under the circumstances."

"Then it shall be," she replies with a sorrowful smile.

She kneels next to the body, as Crundor and Vorrax begin singing a song of sorrow and glory in their tongue. Laying her hands upon Grundel, she begins to chant. Ever so softly her hands begin to glow a fiery red, growing brighter and brighter till they resemble the burning heart of a volcano. The red glow flows from her hands, washing over the body of the fallen dwarf, like lava from that same volcano. When the body is completely engulfed in the all consuming heat flowing from her, it flares, erupts, and is gone. Leaving neither ash, metal, or bone, just a hollowed-out melted spot in the snow and ice.

Rising to her feet, she sways, then collapses in exhaustion. Vorrax, quicker than his stout frame would suggest, scoops her up within his thick arms before she can impact with the snow-covered ground.

"Thank youse, my lady," he says, with a freezing tear on his cheek. "I's is forever in youse debt."

"It was an honor to help such a gallant warrior take his place next to Xax." Wearily she reaches up and wipes the frozen tear from his cheek. "Excuse me my friend, but I need to rest."

"Yes dear lady, I's sorry. Please rest now." Laying her on the ground, he removes his own thick fur cloak and wraps her within it. Then like a mother with a sick child, he fusses over her, making sure she is completely covered and protected from the elements. Finally, he bends over and gently kisses her on the forehead.

Coming over, Elstar lays a hand upon Vorrax, as he watches over the mage. "Come Vorrax, we have things that need to be done before we move on."

Rejoining the gathered group, Elstar addresses them. "We need to hide the bodies of the worgs and cover up all signs of the battle. We can't be sure we weren't seen from a distance. All we can do is cover the bodies with snow, disguising them as snow mounds, and hope that if we were noticed, the snowfall will cover our tracks of departure."

They begin setting about dragging the dead worg bodies into piles and flinging snow upon them with shields and hands. Then taking their cloaks they rake the area smooth, burying the frozen blood and covering the signs of the struggle.

Upon completion of the task, Elstar goes over to where Vesalin is resting. "My princess, I'm sorry to wake you but we must be going."

"Yes, of course." She replies weakly. "Just help me to my feet."

Extending his hand he helps the mage to her feet. Taking four staggering steps she collapses back to the ground.

Vorrax nearly bowling over Elstar, strides to where Vesalin has fallen and scoops her up once again into his arms. "I's will carry her'es." He states firmly, glaring around daring anyone to proclaim differently. Which of course no one does, seeing the determination of the dwarf.

So they resume their journey heading back off into the night. Three humans, an elf and two dwarves, one cradling the female elf to his chest, as if she was a dearly loved child. Which to Vorrax she had become, even though she was a good one-hundred years older than him.

III

Dak'tari slowly arises from the black fog of unconsciousness. As the veil disappears, hollow ghostly voices swirl around her.

"Where did it come from? Where did it come from?"

"What is it doing here? What is it doing here?"

"How did it get here? How did it get here?"

The voices suddenly start to grow excitable, as Dak'tari's eyes begin to flicker open.

"Wait! Wait!"

"It's alive! It's alive!"

Dak'tari begins to shiver as the temperature around her drops sharply to near freezing, and the shrieking wails grow in agitated intensity.

"It's mine!"

"No, it's mine!"

"No, it's mine! I found it!"

Icy, burning talons, like the hands of death, clutch her ankle and wrist, ripping a scream of agonizing pain from her throat and nearly sending her back into the sweet bliss of oblivion.

"It screams! It screams!" Comes the joyous, cackling, echoing laughter of the two voices.

With superhuman effort, Dak'tari shoves aside the pain and concentrates on reaching her weapon with her free hand. Grasping it, she screams with fury and pain as she brings the weapon around towards the creature holding her wrist. Meeting no resistance, the blade flies from her numbed fingers to clank against an unseen stone wall.

"H a, Ha, Ha, Ha, it tries to bite. Ha, Ha, Ha, Ha, it tries to bite."

"Its teeth are useless against us. Ha, Ha, Ha, Ha. Its teeth are useless against us. Ha, Ha, Ha, Ha."

The screech of agony and impotence that Dak'tari lets out, causes the dust from the ceiling to flutter down in a powdery rain, as two fanged-filled jaws clamp down on her shoulder and calf. Frozen tentacles of pain tear through Dak'tari's body as the lapping and sucking jaws begin to drain the blood from her body.

"It burns! It burns!" The voices yowl, as they instantly release their hold on her.

"What is it? What is it?" The voices ask plaintively, fleeing away from her.

"It's not human. It's not human." The spectral voices wail in disappointment, disbelief, and despair.

"No, she is not." Another voice previously unheard answers, this one deep, solid, and lacking the ghostly aspect of the first two. "Leave us my pets. I have questions for this creature." The temperature around Dak'tari instantly rises as the creatures obey their master's command and leave the area.

As the pain and freezing cold recedes, Dak'tari rolls to her painwracked side and tries to focuses her clouded eyes on this newcomer. It takes a moment before her eyes do clear enough for her to see what appears to be a human male, with a balding head, short gray beard, cut square at the bottom, and wearing red robes with a gold trim, coming towards her.

Dak'tari flinches, expecting another icy touch, as the man reaches down and grabs her by the chin. Relief floods through her as she feels only the cold clammy touch of one long dead instead of the liquid nitrogen grasp of those before him. Turning her face towards him, he peers into her red-flecked eyes. Spotting the anomaly his own eyes widen in surprise. "Who are you? What are you?"

Dak'tari's refusal to answer his questions brings a thin smile to his gray, pallid face. "Should I call my pets back?" His smile growing even wider.

Fear and indecision shake the very fabric of Dak'tari's being. Loss of blood and the chilling numbness, still locked within her bones, makes her too weak to pull her chin from his hand, not to mention launch some kind of attack. *What am I to do?* The little girl that is Dak'tari pleads. *If I can't I get away, I will fail my beloved.*

"Who is your beloved?" The man demands, roughly shaking her head.

With horror, Dak'tari realizes that he can hear her thoughts.

"That's right my pet." He sneers. "So you can tell me what I wish to know or I can rip it from you. And if you thought my pets' touch was painful, just wait till I start tearing through your most inner thoughts."

"Screw you!" Dak'tari spits.

The laugh that comes from the mage's dead throat contains no mirth but only rancid amusement. "No my dear, screw you." And with that, he plunges into Dak'tari's mind as if he was kicking in a thin wooden door to an unholy sanctum.

The pain is like red hot irons violently thrust into tender young flesh, as the ripping, twisting, searching tentacles plunge into the swirling mass of Dak'tari's memories. A sound seems to come to her from way afar and at first, she is not sure what they are; then as they become more distinct, she wonders who is making those horrid screams, never realizing they are coming from her own throat.

A psychedelic tornado of colors and images whirls through her mind. Some are clasped by the searching tentacles dragged to the forefront, observed, and then cast aside, allowing the questing fingers to clasp others. Then one is grabbed and held, while the mage watches intently. It seems strange to her because it is not one of her memories, it was one of those given to her by her beloved.

A black-clad figure stands over a creature on the verge of giving birth. Whipping out a sword, the figure lops off the head of the pregnant creature, before kneeling, slitting open its› belly and removing the squirming baby within.

The images go black as the tentacles yank back in surprise. "Your mother was a succubus!" Disbelief drips from the mage's awed voice. "That's why your blood burned my pets. But why? Why would someone breed with a devil?" Then as if struck by lightning, the possibilities send him reeling. "Can it be? Can it truly be? Show me, Show me more! Who is your beloved?" He demands before delving back into her mind.

Memories come into focus, scanned, evaluated, and then left in the darkness as he moves to the next. Images of her childhood flitter past, scenes of monotonous nothingness, such as being bathed, fed, and being taken care of by Cantanis in the Black Fortress. The images whirl on searching, seeking for something of interest. They again come to a stop on the image of Dak'tari as a little girl.

Dak'tari reaches out her arm, pointing to a black stiletto hanging on the wall. An old man lifts her to grab the weapon, then sets her upon an altar. The old man then plucks a hair from Dak'tari's head, wraps it within a ball, and feeds it to a little white dog. The dog then goes insane and leaps for her throat. Stunned, Dak'tari is knocked to the floor, then something.

"What was that! Someone spoke to you! Someone else has been in your mind before! Show me, damn you, show me who!"

She plunges the blade into the puppy's heart killing him. The old man lifts Dak'tari and the puppy and sets them on the altar. The old man slaps Dak'tari telling her to cut the dog's head off and give it to him. She hesitates, then the voice again.

"Damn it, girl! Who is it? Show me, show me NOW!!!!!"

Dak'tari sits on the floor of a small room. A raging wind begins to swirl around her and lifts her from the ground. Then a gently sweet voice starts to speak to her.

"Yes! Yes!" This is what he is looking for. Then His leering grin of ecstasy changes to a contorted grimace of pain and horror. Claws of flaming terror sear into his mind as a voice from the deepest pit of hell explodes within his brain.

"So you wished to see that which was not meant for you? Well, instead see that which is!"

The wailing shriek that emerges from the mage contains all the torturous torment of a wretched soul being burned alive at the stake. Blistering flames consume his dead flesh, his eyeballs pop, melt, and flow down his cheeks in a gooey mass. His mind begins to teeters on the brink of insanity as his flesh starts to melt away in a bulbous, oozing, waxy mess. Then as if covered with the cooling, lapping waves of the ocean the pain is gone.

"Now, pathetic mage," comes the voice of Uthanor. "You have two choices. We can restart the pain and I can leave you like that all time, or you can serve me. What is your choice?"

Balled up in a corner, in the fetal position, the mage grovels. "No! No more pain, please. I will do whatever you ask."

The mirthful laugh of Uthanor chills the mage's, unbeaten heart. "Wise choice. This is what I require of you." Sharp burning pain like a bolt to the brain pierces his skull. "Do you understand what I require of you?"

"Yes my lord, I will do as you desire."

"Good. Serve me well and you shall be rewarded. Betray me and the torment you felt before shall be nothing." Then Uthanor's voice brushes against the mind of Dak'tari and is gone.

Rising to her feet, Dak'tari limps over to where the mage still lays huddled in the corner and punches him in his gray pasty face. Turning she limps back across the chamber to where her stiletto lays upon the floor. It flies from her hand, like a black lightning bolt, and is embedded in the wall a hairsbreadth from his head, quivering like an angry hornet.

Trembling with fury, she yanks her blade from the wall. "If my beloved had not told me you were useful I would kill you this instant."

Instantly the air around Dak'tari drops in temperature announcing the return of the mages' so-called pets. "Call them off!" Immediately the black blade is shoved beneath his beard and pressed against his neck.

"Stop!" He commands his wraiths. "It's alright. She is on my side, or I should say I'm on her side." Reaching up slowly he places an index finger on the blade at his throat and smiles at someone with an amusing secret. "Child, your blade will not work on me. I'm already dead and on the plane of death. So, therefore your weapon cannot affect me." With the speed of a rattlesnake, he grabs the blade and shoves it through his neck. "See." He says with a macabre laugh, as the blade tip sticks out of the opposite side of his neck.

In disbelief, Dak'tari removes the blade from the mage's neck and plops upon the floor. In dejection, her head slumps into the palms of her hands. "How am I suppose to kill that which is already dead?"

A cold clammy hand grasp her shoulder in an awkward attempt at comfort. "I believe, I can help you with that."

"How?"

"You truly know nothing about yourself and the powers you possess?" It was not a question, but more a statement of disbelief. He falls silent for a moment in contemplation. Then he slowly nods his head as his glassy eyes crystallize in understanding. "Yes, yes I see. We were meant to cross paths. Your dark lord is more cunning than I first believed." He throws back his head, laughing with the gusto and abandon of one long blind whose sight has suddenly been restored.

"What's so funny?" Dak'tari demands, rising to her feet. Her fist clenched in anger at the thought that he was laughing at her ignorance.

"Child, did you not feel as if you were being guided towards me?"

"So? What if I was. Why you?"

"Because I can help you unlock the demon's blood that flows through your veins." Turning he starts walking down a passage. "Here, follow me."

Following the mage, favoring her injured leg, he leads her to a larger chamber connected to the one they are in. With a wave of his hand, he indicates that Dak'tari should take a seat in one of the four chairs in this new room.

"How can you do that?" She asks doubtfully. "What could you possibly know of demon-kind and how their blood works?"

"Because child, I devoted my life," a sarcastic smile touches his pallid features, "when I was alive, that is, to the study of Demonology. My name is, was, whatever..." He waves a hand dismissively. "Nephlyngard the Red."

"So what. I don't have time for this. I have things I need to do." Rising Dak'tari turns to leave.

"Sit!" Anger spews from Nephlyngard like a sun flare. "Are you so foolish as to believe you're just going to walk up to the Gauntlar and cut his head off? I already proved to you that you can not kill the dead on the plane of death. Do you think that excludes the lord of death himself?" Dak'tari pauses as his words sink in. "Now are you going to sit or do I need to call my pets and make you sit? Your lord told me to instruct you in what you needed to know and that's what I'm going to do."

"Good, very good." He says as Dak'tari returns to her seat. "To answer your first concern," he begins, taking on the air of a college professor. "You have all the time in the world. Time is meaningless here. What feels like a hundred years could be no more than a minute on Tamora, and what feels like a minute could be a hundred years. It is a matter of perspective. This is a realm of the mind, not the body. So, it is more of a matter of when you want it to be, than the actual number of sunrises and sunsets on Tamora." He pauses to see if Dak'tari understands, but from the confused look on her face, he realizes that she does not quite grasp the concept. Shaking his head in dismissal, he adds. "It is not important that you understand the concept or not. Just know that time has no meaning here. Our main concern is that your presence here is not detected by Gauntlar."

"This will keep me from being detected." Dak'tari proudly indicates her suit of dark-elf flesh.

"Do you not realize what you are dealing with?" Anger and frustration drip from his voice in a black ickor. "You are not dealing with a mortal! You are dealing with a god! A god on his plane! Even now he probably senses your life force in his domain! Now, yank your head out of your ass! Put your stupid, prideful naivete aside and learn what I have to teach you, or you will fail your lord!"

Dak'tari springs to her feet, her anger dwarfing the mages. "How dare you talk to me like this! I am the chosen of my beloved!"

"Enough of this shit!" Nephlyngard cries. "Take her!"

Dak'atri howls in pain as the freezing hands of the wraiths seize her and fling her back into the seat, holding her in place.

"I was hoping this would not be necessary. But I see now it is as I was shown. You are just a child, and a spoiled child at that, in a woman's body. So you need to be instructed as a spoiled child does." Reaching out he seizes her face in an iron grip. He's dead, milkywhite eyes bore into her. "And that means with the lash if need be." Releasing her, he walks from the chamber into another room. As he leaves, his parting words send a tremor of fear coursing through her. "See if you can make her more pliable, by the time I return my pets." And then the screaming started.

Eventually, the screaming subsides as Nephlyngard returns back into the room. With a flick of his wrist, the wraiths let loose of their hold on Dak'tari and retreat off into the darkness.

"So my sweet, are you ready to learn what I have to teach you?" A barely perceptible nod is her only reply. "Good. We shall begin with what you probably need to know the most right now. The ability to regenerate."

Again assuming the attitude of the college professor, he begins to instruct Dak'tari in the ability to regenerate. "Now as you may or may not know regeneration is an innate ability of demon-kind. But due to the fact that you have human blood flowing through your veins, it has suppressed this natural ability that comes to full-blooded demon-kind upon spawning. Now what we must do is force your demon blood to overcome the constraints of your human blood."

"And how are we supposed to do that?" Dak'tari asks weakly.

A sinister sneer spreads across Nephlyngard's face. "By stripping off your clothes and giving me your weapon."

"What?" She vomits." Do you take me for a fool?" Rage and indignation again swell her form. "I will never relinquish my weapon." The thought of standing naked before this walking corpse was not a concern of hers at all. But the idea of freely giving up her weapon was totally and completely out of the question.

"As I said before. We don't have time for this." With a resigned sigh, he summons the wraiths back. Instantly she is seized, stripped, thrown in the chair, and bound securely to it. Her weapon rises from the floor, where it had fallen while being striped, and seemingly floats through the air, carried by the hand of one of the invisible wraiths, and set into Nephlyngard's waiting hand.

Bellowing in rage, Dak'tari thrashes and bucks against her bonds trying to free herself. Finally, she slumps back in exhaustion. Panting she gasps, "So now you kill me?"

"You are a fool!" Nephlyngard hisses, slapping her across the face and splitting her lip.

As the metallic taste of her blood touches her taste buds, she rolls it upon her tongue before spitting it back in his face, focusing all her hate and anger on that tiny red arrow.

As the spittle drips down Nephlyngard's face, like a bloody tear he leans down next to Dak'tari and whispers into her ear. "To answer your question. Yes, I do think you a fool." He pauses a moment. "But that will change." He adds, slowly almost lovely sliding her black blade into her shoulder.

For the next three hours that black stiletto, which was Dak'tari's pride and joy, plunged in and out of her soft, white flesh like a gruesome lover. With each wound inflicted and drop of blood released she could feel her life force slowly slipping away. All through the torture session, Dak'tari realizes that the mage is very careful not to hit any vital organs or inflict a grievous enough wound as to cause instant death. In a morbid way Dak'tari admires his skill at the art of inflicting pain before nearly drained of blood, she slips into unconsciousness.

A whispering voice comes to her, as if from a hundred miles away, at first she can't make out the words nor does she care. She just wanted to fall asleep and let the tide of death carry her upon its gently lapping waves, slip under its waters, and have them close over her head and be engulfed into its awaiting depths.

The voice grows stronger, more persistent, calling her back like a hand thrust into those waters and pulling her to the surface. "Good. Yes, very good. Feel the pain ease away. Feel the blood of your mother course through your veins, repairing the damage to your body."

As the voice grows stronger a miraculous transformation overcomes her tortured body, under the intent gaze of Nephlyngard, who watches her as if she was a test subject in a laboratory, which to him that was exactly what she was. First, like erosion in reverse, the cuts start to knit themselves back together. Then with ever-increasing speed, her blood ceases to flow, becoming first a trickle then stopping altogether. Her ripped, cut and torn flesh binds itself, becoming a jagged torn wound. Followed by a red inflamed scar, the pink rubbery stamp of a freshly healed wound, then vanishing completely without the trace of a mark.

Dak'tari's eyes flicker, blinded momentarily by the dim light in the stone chamber, before focusing on the smiling face of Nephlyngard before her.

"Well that wasn't so difficult, was it?" He says, removing the ropes holding her to the chair.

Like a bolt of lightning, Dak'tari lashes out seizing the smiling mage by the throat and pinning him against the wall. "You bastard! I'll rip you..."

The laughter of Nephlyngard interrupts her. "Tsk, tsk my dear. Have we not been through this already? There is nothing you can do or threaten me with here. Think child, think. Don't you realize what just happened?"

"Yes, you piece of shit! You just tried to kill me!"

"Are you sure? Then why are you not dead? Why is it you can stand here now, trying to squeeze the life out of a lifeless throat?" His smile broadens as he sees the dawning of comprehension slowing starting to seep in.

"Can it be?" She whispers to herself, as her limp fingers slip from the mage's throat. "How?"

"By placing you in such a condition that your demon blood was forced to rise to the surface to save you or let you die. I don't expect you to understand. Just know..."

"But I do! That explains the air, and the water," she blurts excitedly.

"What air? What water? What are you.." He stops in mid-sentence, nodding his head in understanding. "Yes, I see. I didn't even think about the fact that you should not be able to breathe here. So you must of went through something similar when you first arrived on this plane, yes." She begins to relate to him her experiences with the air and water when she first arrived on the plane.

Nephlyngard listens intently while she talks, interjecting now and then with a question or nod of his head. When she is done he finally speaks. "As I explained before, demon spawn is born with natural innate abilities. But since you are half-demon your innate abilities will only manifest themselves when your body is in extreme duress. Hence the ability to free-breathe in an oxygen-free environment. I would surmise that you can now probably breathe underwater and in a poison-rich atmosphere. As for the water, that is a surprising bonus. Especially concerning our next stage."

"What do you mean?"

"The ability to create water, and food for that matter, is a spell." The mage begins to explain. "Not a very powerful spell, but a spell nonetheless. The ability to cast spells may seem the same, but it is vastly different."

"Now demons, of course, can cast spells, but it comes later in their existence. Some spells come a lot easier to one type of demon than to others. In other words, some can cast lightning bolts a lot easier than they can cast, let's say fireballs and vice-a-versa. But as I said before, that ability usually comes later in their existence. So, therefore, I must surmise that your dark lord unlocked that ability when he took you within his embrace. He must know, as do I, that there is only one way to destroy Gauntlar on his plane, and that is with a spell cast by a half-mortal in a very special location."

"What spell, where?" Dak'tari asks anxiously.

"Patience child, I shall explain all in due time."

"Now then, the spell is an extremely powerful one, and can only be cast by the most powerful of demon-kind. Hopefully, your dark lord has granted you the ability to cast spells far beyond a younglings ability. But, our biggest problem is you must learn the reverse of it." He pauses as he rises to his feet and heads towards the other room.

"Rest now. There are things I need to review and prepare. I have to make sure the wards of obfuscation are still active. Bringing you so close to death would have surely notified Gauntlar as to your whereabouts if not for them. I'm sure he sensed your life force since you arrived on the planes of dust and wind. I would have to guess that your suit did help in keeping your location from him though. I can only hope that he doesn't think to look for you here, at least until we are ready."

Left alone, Dak'tari puts back on her suit of skin and reviews all the things he has told her. Finally, she decides understanding is not overly important to her, only action. She then falls asleep.

Sometime later Dak'tari is awoken by a cold chill surrounding her. Instantly she is awake and on her feet.

"Master says come," commands one wraith.

"Master says come," echoes the second.

Quickly she crosses the chamber, glad to get away from the wraith chilling touch, and enters the room that Nephlyngard had entered upon his departure.

Littering the room in apparent haphazard disarray were countless tomes, scrolls, and various magical diagrams and charts covering the tables, chairs, shelves, floor and secured to the walls.

Dak'tari treads her way through the magical clutter and approaches the mage, who is bent over, pouring through a book laying on the table before him.

"Are you ready?" Nephlyngard asks, refusing to pull his nose from out of the book.

"Yes," Dak'tari replies simply.

Placing his finger on the page, to mark his spot, he lifts his eyes and faces Dak'tari. "You will only have one chance to cast this spell. Neither will you be able to practice it before you cast it against Gauntlar, otherwise he would sense it. So you must learn it perfectly. Do you understand?"

"Yes. Just let us begin."

For the next four periods of sleep, for that was the only way Dak'tari had any indication of the passage of time, Nephlyngard tutored her in the casting of the spell. At some points, it seemed as if she had remained awake for weeks before he would let her sleep. During those times of never-ending wakefulness, the mage taught her the intricate wording, inflections, and gestures of the spell. Scolding her severely when she messed up, and just nodding his head and moving on to the next step when she got it correct.

After the grueling days, weeks, or whatever it was, of preparation, Nephlyngard finally gives his assent. "Well child, your as ready as I can prepare you. You know what you need to do, yes?"

"Let's do it!" She says, full of anticipation.

"Yes, let's." He replies with a sinister sneer. Unexpectedly Dak'tari is seized by the chilling hands of the wraiths. The shock of the betrayal and the agony of the wraith's grip is like an avalanche tumbling over her leaving her stunned, chilled, and speechless.

Seizing her face, his fetid breath washed over her in his laughter. "Foolish child, did you believe I could betray my true master?"

Releasing her, he turns and goes to a section of the wall covered with a diagram containing some kind of magical emblem. Removing it from the wall with a violent tug, he places his hand on the bared surface. His fingers begin to dance in an intricate pattern upon the wall, causing a section to slide back revealing a small alcove. Within the exposed space stands a slime-covered basin filled with foul-smelling rancid water. As he waves his hand over the basin putrid fog begins to arise from water, coalescing into a wavering, pulsating skull with sickly purplish glowing eyes.

"Nephlyngard," comes a croaking, raspy voice from the skull, sounding as if it was clawing its way out of the earth from a thousand graves. "Why have you disturbed me?"

He prostrates himself before the specter of Gauntlar. "Forgive me my lord, but I have a gift for you."

"What could you possibly have for me?" A tinge of anger begins to infuse the voice.

"A mortal." The mage replies, still prostrate on the floor.

"A mortal! A mortal!" The anger in the voice becomes a raging flow of lava ready to sweep all before its' wrath. "How dare you bother me with such triviality! All mortals come to me in time! You will spend the rest of eternity screaming for this disturbance!"

"Please my lord." Nephlyngard pleads before the wrath of the death god. "This is no ordinary mortal, she is the one that destroyed your high priest."

The anger is replaced from the voice with chilling contempt. "Where is this sacrilegious sack of flesh?"

Rising to his feet Nephlyngard beckons to his wraiths to drag a kicking and screaming Dak'tari forward. "Here my lord."

"You have her?" Comes the very pleasing voice of Gauntlar. "Bring her to me immediately. I shall send Mordigon for you and the infidel. You shall be greatly rewarded for this Nephlyngard."

"Thank you, my lord. We shall be waiting." Nephlyngard says bowing graciously, as the foggy skull dissipates.

Turning from the alcove Nephlyngard returns to the anti-chamber, followed by the two wraiths dragging Dak'tari between them. Heading up a passage, hidden behind an outcropping of rock, they wind their way along till they come to an exit. Stepping out, they enter a world with the same haunting appearance as the landscape Dak'tari first appeared in. Except on this side of the mountain range, the wind does not stir at all, not the slightest breeze disturbs dust or sky. The air is as still and stagnant as that found in a long-lost tomb left undisturbed for eons.

IV

By the time the weak, bleary sun peaked its shadowed head over the horizon, the group finds themselves making their way up the steep incline of a black, ice-scarred mountain. They tread their way up the winding trail, which zigs and zags like the sand-strewn path of a sidewinder, their heads bowed and bodies braced against the blistering wind. At each step the wind howls and screams in protest, doing its damnedest to knock them from the ledge and send them tumbling to their doom. Rounding a bend in the trail, near the peaking ridge which obscures the rest of the trail, Elstar calls a halt.

"We're being followed," states the elf.

"Four orcs from what I can tell," replies Deramar with a supporting arm wrapped around Vesalin

"You have good eyes Deramar. That's my count also."

"I believe Darl and I can handle this scum if that's alright with you captain," Deramar says, looking at Dyrgen for approval, who nods his head.

"We shall continue on while you and Darl conceal yourselves here. If you haven't caught up with us by the time we reach the bottom, we will set up camp and wait for you there," instructs Elstar.

"We shall meet you there," replies Deramar.

Vesalin comes up to Deramar and takes his face in her hands. "Be careful my love," she whispers before kissing him.

Smiling reassuringly, he folds her within his arm. "Don't worry my love, all will be well."

While the remainder of the group makes their way over the peak and down the trail, Darl and Deramar begin preparing their places of concealment. Placing themselves about fifteen feet apart, they begin scooping the snow away from the rock wall face. Laying down within the indention's, they pull the snow back over themselves and wait.

After thirty or so minutes, they hear the crunching footsteps of the orcs coming up the trail.

"The general says the time is near." Comes the gruff voice of one of the orcs.

"Yes, general says they are not to reach the gathering point, says another.

"They won't. Stupid fair skins no match for us" replies a third.

"Yes, stupid fair skin not realizes general travel with them. When army ready, land of fair skins be ours. Ha,ha,ha." Laughs the voice of the first orc.

Then we shall feast on their flesh and suck the sweet marrow from their bones," comes the voice of the third orc, sending his companions into a fit of lustful laughter.

"Shut up fools!" Comes the commanding voice of the fourth orc, "Something wrong."

The sound of sniffing triggers Deramar and Darl into action. Springing from their cover in a flurry of snow and weapons the two humans dispatch two of the orcs in the first stunned seconds of surprise.

Ripping his war-pick from out of the ore he has just killed, Darl swings it upwards, puncturing another orc's groin and burying his weapon deep within its guts, turning a war howl into a girlish screech. Darl then turns to find Deramar watching him through slitted eyes, with the commander of the orcs standing calmly next to him.

"It was you, they were talking about." Darl stammers, sudden understanding flooding his eyes.

"Yes." Deramar smiles menacingly. "I needed you so I could get into Xaxtor and see what kind of defenses they had. And also to find out how much the three kingdoms knew. Frankly, I was a little surprised that fool of a Dyrgen accepted me so quickly, I thought I would have to work a lot harder to gain his confidence. I guess setting up that ambush back in the woods and that bullshit story of Pasadera was enough though. Just between us, I helped cause that civil war, it will make Pasadera too weak to fight against us in the coming war. Hell, Fairinan will probably come in on our side. Anyway, now that I have accomplished what I needed, I have no more use for you."

"You son of a bitch!" Darl growls, lifting his pick and charging Deramar.

Deramar blocks the incoming blow with ease, turning it to the side. Laughing he taunts Darl, "I never knew my mother, but I have no doubts she was." With a flick of his wrist, he sends Darl's pick wide, spins, and thrusts his sword through Darl's exposed stomach. With a twist, slice and a yank the knight gazes down in disbelief as his intestines fall upon the snow, staining the pure whiteness a gory red.

"Quickly kill him! Crush his skull now!" Deramar orders the remaining orc.

Without hesitation, the ore rushes forward and brings his spiked club down with a meaty thump upon the disemboweled knight's head. Turning from his handy work, the orc is greeted by the choking clasp of Deramar's hand around his throat. The glare from Deramar's eyes contains no hint of humanity. Issuing instructions, he releases the strangled orc with a shove. "Make sure you are not seen, or the last moment of your life will be long and painful. Do you understand?"

"Yes general," stammers the ore chieftain, rubbing his blackish-green neck.

"Now I want you to stab me."

"What?" Asks the confused orc, believing he had heard incorrectly.

"I said to stab me! Do you think those fools down there are going to believe that four orcs killed Darl, and I didn't get injured at all? I need them to believe enough of my story that they will want to check for themselves and while they are distracted with me, it will give you the chance to do as I ordered. Now stab me, here!" He orders again, slapping a hand to his shoulder.

"Yes general, as you command." The orc replies confused but obeying with a quick thrust of his dagger.

"Now go, and do not fail me!" Deramar orders, placing a hand over the wound to staunch the bleeding.

"I will not fail you general. All shall be as you order."

"It better be!" The orc then turns and races back down the path to do his general's bidding.

Catching up to the waiting group, camping in a cave bored into the mountain, Deramar staggers into the opening with blood flowing through his fingers and down his side. Collapsing the falls onto the floor of the enclosure. Gasping in anxiety, Vesalin rushes up to her injured lover, as Dyrgen and Elstar step outside looking around expectantly for Darl. As the minutes slip past without any sign of the knight, they return to the sheltering protection of the cave.

"Where is Darl!" Dyrgen demands of Deramar, who given a healing draught by Vesalin, lays cradled on her lap while the potion takes effect.

"Where is Darl!" Dyrgen demands again.

"Leave him alone!" Flares Vesalin protectively. "He's injured, can't you let him heal?"

"It's alright my love," Deramar says soothingly, rising to his feet to stand before Dyrgen. "I'm sorry Captain. He's dead." The sorrow in his eyes echoes through his voice.

"Bullshit!" Dyrgen flares in anger. "There is no damn way four orcs could kill Darl! He was the best knight I had! Shit! I've seen him kill ten orcs single-handed!"

As the Captain of the Reatha Knights raves at Deramar, Elstar, Vorrax, and Crundor encircle Deramar, disbelief at Dari's fall shows clearly on their faces.

"What are you doing?" Vesalin proclaims, searching the faces of the enclosing mob. "You don't believe Deramar had something to do with Darl's death?" She asks incredulously, moving to stand defensively next to her lover.

Placing a comforting hand on her shoulder Deramar gently but persuasively guides her behind him. "Of course they do, and I can not blame them. Darl was a great and powerful warrior. His death was a heavy and tragic blow for all the company." His eyes lock with each of his companions standing before him, moving from one to another. "What can I do to prove my innocence?"

"Not a damn ..." Dyrgen begins before being interrupted by Elstar.

"There is one thing. Vesalin you know what I speak of."

"And if I refuse?" The mage states defiantly.

"You won't," Deramar says stroking her flushed cheek. "Do as he wishes, if that's what it takes to alleviate their suspicions."

With tears of anguish running down her cheeks, she reaches into a pouch on her side removing a tiny amount of powder. Lifting her hand above his head, she sprinkles the powder upon him. As it drifts down she starts to chant. Upon completion, she turns on the group. "There," She says angrily. "If he lies a blue aura will form around him."

"Now, Deramar," Demands Elstar. "Tell us what happened upon the peak?"

"Darl and I," Deramar begins. "Took refuse in the snow, scooping out holes next to the rock face and pulling it back over us. It wasn't too long before the ores approached. They must have sensed something was wrong because they came to a halt right by us and started to sniff the air. It was then that we sprung the trap. Darl fought like a lion, slaying two of the beast while I slew one. Then he fell, struck through the stomach. Then before my eyes, the last orc crushed his skull killing him." The memory of that moment seems to fill his eyes full of sorrow and regret. "Turning to me the orc stuck me in the shoulder with his dagger. I then dispatched the orc and made my way here." Finishing his tale, he falls silent. At no point did the magical powder flair.

"See," Vesalin says dispelling the detect lie spell. "He was telling the truth. He had nothing to do with Darl's death."

"So it would seem," replies Elstar. "I'm sorry Deramar for doubting you. And I'm sorry about Darl, Dyrgen, he was a brave warrior and will be sorely missed."

"I too, am very sorry Captain. I did everything I could to save him." Deramar says regretfully, as his foot quickly shifts a fraction of an inch, covering the weak blue glowing speck on the floor.

Nodding his head, Dyrgen walks out into the snow to be left alone with his grief.

Deramar, enfolding Vesalin within the folds of his cloak, leads her to the farthest reaches of the cavern. The elf and two dwarves gaze at the falling snow, its' icy coldness reflecting the chilling dread that blankets their hearts.

"This does not bode well," Elstar says clenching his fist. "Two of our party dead, one sent home and another enthralled by..." His voice trails off, falling into silence.

"So youse don't believe Deramar's story?" Vorrax asks.

"Something doesn't add up. You've seen Deramar and Darl both fight, I just can't believe that four orcs could slay one and wound another without some kind of assistance. Yet what he said was the truth. I know Vesalin cast her spell correctly. Besides, I don't believe she would condone such a betrayal if she knew that was the case. So, I say again, he was telling the truth, yet something doesn't add up."

The dwarf nods his head in agreement. "I's was thinking along those same lines. What do youse think we's should do?"

"Nothing. We do nothing except keep a very close eye on Deramar, till we have proof one way or another."

"Aye. It will be as youse say. I's think we's should go see about Dyrgen. We's still have a job to do. Even if we's do possibly have a spider in our's midst."

"Your right, we need to be moving out soon. Let us go and retrieve our grieving friend." Pulling their cloaks tightly about themselves, they step out of the cave and into the falling snow; leaving Crundor to watch over the cave and Vesalin if necessary.

As Elstar and Vorrax trail after Dyrgen, Deramar kisses the top of Vesalin head as it rests on top of his chest, their bodies intertwined underneath their thick furs.

"Thank you," he whispers into her blonde hair

"For what my love?" She sighs, snuggling closer, seemingly in an effort to become one body as they were one heart.

"For believing me."

"Of course I believe you. I love you," she huskily replies.

She kisses him deeply with a fierce undying passion. "Besides I don't think I care."

Smiling with inner satisfaction he returns her kiss.

*****

Following Dyrgen's path, Elstar and Vorrax locate him on the mountain peak, next to a cairn of stone containing Darl's body.

"We need to be moving on Dyrgen." Elstar says, placing a sympathetic hand on Dyrgen's shoulder.

"Look," says Vorrax. "Do youse see anything wrong?"

"What do you mean?" Asks Elstar, glancing around the area.

A throaty growl comes from next to the cairn. "There are only three dead orcs." Hisses the infuriated knight, tearing his sword from his side and heading back down the mountain. "I noticed when I got here. I wanted to give Darl a proper burial, and now it's time for Deramar to explain himself. To my sword!"

*****

Hand in hand Deramar and Vesalin return from their seclusion at the back of the cave, to find it empty except for Crundor.

"Where are the others?" Asks Vesalin, looking around in wonder.

"Gone to find Dyrgen," the dwarf replies, eyeing Deramar warily.

"Hmm," Deramar says smiling slyly. "Where did they go, I wonder."

"I's would guess back to the mountaintop," answers Crundor.

"But why?" Asks Vesalin.

"To see if I was telling the truth or not." Deramar answers.

"But my spell showed you were telling the truth."

"They had their doubts. I expected they would want to go see for themselves."

"But why?" Vesalin repeats, confused.

"It's O.K. my love. All shall be made clear shortly." Deramar says soothingly as if calming an upset child.

"What. . . what do you mean?" She asks frantically staring at Deramar, desperately trying to grasp what is happening.

Crundor hefting his ax, eyeing Deramar, trying to decipher his cryptic words. "What shall be made clear?"

Derarnar leaning against the wall, placidly answers. "That must wait till the others get back."

"Youse will tell me now!" The dwarf demands, stepping forward and brandishing his ax.

The cold, dead, heartlessness of the human's eyes freezes the blood of the dwarf, drawing him up short. "I said we will wait." He whispers in a tone that brokers no dispute, leaving the dwarf afraid. Afraid in such a way as he has never felt or thought he ever could.

Vesalin pressed in a corner, cradles her face in her hands, and begins to weep. The sobs and tears are those of a lost and confused child, heartbroken, alone, and desperately trying to comprehend what was going on around her, as all her hopes and dreams seem to be turning into dust and slipping through her tear-stained fingers.

For long moments the cave is silent, except for the sobs of Vesalin. Deramar leaning against the wall, his head slumps upon his chest, breaths deeply in apparent sleep. While Crundor standing mute, eyeing the resting human, quivers in anger, fear, and indecision.

Then the silence is ripped asunder as Dyrgen returns fuming in rage and screaming for the blood of Deramar, followed closely by Elstar and Vorrax.

"Deramar!" Bellows Dyrgen. "You traitorous, lying, son of a whore! Prepare to meet my sword and your death!" Then he charges Deramar, passing the immobile Crundor, like a maddened bull thrusting for the blood of a matador.

As the blade of the knight arcs downward toward the still unmoving Deramar, a shrill scream of denial erupts from the back of the cave. Dyrgen, lifted from his feet, is flung like a broken rag doll to slam against the wall. First gapping at his smoldering chest in disbelief, he raises his head to stare in dumbfounded wonder at Vesalin, whose hands outstretched still trail ghostly wisps of smoke from the spell she just cast.

Dyrgen, Elstar, and Vorrax so intent on their revenge, and Crundor who stood rooted to the floor like a great oak, had failed to notice that two ice boulders had appeared next to the cave entrance where no boulders had been before. Enthralled by the scene before them, they fail to notice that the two snow-covered, blue crystalline ice boulders now rise behind them to become two ice trolls.

Fifteen feet of rock-hard water, they are thin but contain immense strength, with teeth and claws resembling sharply pointed icicles which can rip through flesh and steel, like an iceberg through the hull of a ship. Huge angular heads, grinning with lustful malice, sit atop long, thin necks, jutting forward and looking as if they are about to go head over heels.

The thundering crunch of the trolls' footsteps alerts the elf and dwarves to the danger coming up from behind them. Spinning, Vorrax greets one with the gleaming edge of his axe, shattering three of its fingers and removing a fist-sized chunk from a thigh as it reaches for him. Without the slightest indication of pain, it backhands the dwarf with its good hand, sending him flying across the cave.

Elstar rapidly fires three arrows within the blink of an eye, which bounce off the creature's rock-hard chest, causing nothing more than a few flecks of ice to fly off. Realizing the futility of the elf's arrows against the ice creature, Crundor charges forward with a war cry and embeds his axe into its exposed side, sending a rippling crack running through the troll's body with an ear-popping snap. Enraged, the troll howls in pain and slams a hand, fingers extended, through Crundor's face. Blood and brains splatter through the air in a crimson shower and drip from its fingers as it extracts its hand from the mangled face of the dwarf, before taking one shuddering step and collapsing into a thousand fragments.

Vorrax, shaking off the impact with the wall, rushes back into the fray with the surviving troll in a whirling dervish of steel and curses.

With the remaining troll engaged, Elstar turns his attention to Deramar, who still appears completely undisturbed by the fighting going on around him. Raising his bow, he carefully aims an arrow at the sleeping human and fires.

Shock and dismay fill the elf's eyes as Deramar's hand deftly snatches the arrow from out of the air and snaps it between two fingers. Dropping the arrow Deramar rises to his feet, drawing his sword. "So I guess this means it's your turn?" He says with a sarcastically tragic tinge.

Deramar slowly and deliberately makes his way towards Elstar, easily blocking two more arrows with his blade. Then as if by magic he stands before the elf, his sword sweeping downward, severing the elf's bow in half. Before Elstar can react, the tip of the blade is pressed beneath his chin and caressing his jugular.

The elf prepares himself for the death which he is sure to come when the tip of Deramar's blade drops from his throat.

"As a show of respect, Elstar." Deramar says sincerely. "I will allow you to die with a weapon in your hand. Draw your sword." With a bow of his head, Deramar backs up, allowing the elf room to maneuver.

Momentarily stunned Elstar doesn't move, sure that this is some sort of trick. But as Deramar stands patiently before him, he reaches to his side and draws his sword.

The two blades meet in the air in a shower of sparks. Thrust after slash after thrust are all parried by Deramar, as Elstar presses the attack. Pressing his advantage, the elf steadily drives the human back. Feeling the thrill of victory, the elf's blows come quicker and quicker, but each time they are met by Deramar's sword and turned aside. As Elstar's arm starts to grow heavy a dawning realization begins to take hold.

"Stop...toying...with...me." The elf demands through labored breathing.

"As you wish," Deramar replies obligingly, as his sword slips past Elstar's guard and plunges into his heart.

It seemed funny to Elstar that his last thought should be how strange it was for him to be so exhausted and yet Deramar had not even broken a sweat. Then he thinks nothing at all, as he slides off Deramar's sword, dead.

As Deramar and Elstar performed their dance of death, Vorrax continues his struggle with the ice troll, battered, bruised, and bleeding from several wounds. Some were minor, others leaving him halfblind from the loss of an eye and his left arm dangling broken and useless. Vorrax twist rolls and continues to chop at the slowly diminishing troll.

Leaning like a collapsing megalith, from the lack of a leg below the knee, the troll fights on with the savage fury of an ice age. Swiping a hand with only two claws remaining at the dwarf, it collapses into splinters as Vorrax ducking under the swing, shatters its skull with a blow from his axe held within his remaining good hand.

As Vorrax claws, his way out of the shattered remains, he is greeted by the glimmering tip of Deramar 's sword. "Very impressive show Vorrax, but it ends now."

Deramar pauses as Vesalin's voice comes to him in a whisper, finally released from the catatonic state which has held her since she struck down Dyrgen. "Deramar. Please, I beg you, don't kill him."

Walking past the bloody and icy mayhem, strewn upon the floor, she places a quivering restraining hand gently upon his arm. "If you spare him, I will go with you. You and I can just go. We can make a life together away from everything, just you and I."

The cold heartless laughter that answers her is a cruel slap in the face. Destroying all the beauty, hopes, and dreams that were contained within her pure golden soul. "What makes you think I care?"

"It was all a lie. Everything was a lie. She cries incredulously, as tears of betrayal roll down her face.

Before the first tear slides from her flushed cheeks to splash upon the floor, Deramar's sword sweeps around in a full circle and severs the dwarf's and his lover's head nearly simultaneously. Both of them smack to the ground with a grisly, sickening thump, rock back and forth, and come to rest within inches of each other, staring wide-eyed into each others slowly glazing orbs.

Bending down, Deramar wipes his bloody sword clean on Vesalin robes, lifts her head, brushes back her golden hair, and delicately kisses her still warm lips. "Ah, my love. If it is any consolation, you were amusing." Laughing, he unceremoniously drops her head and walks out of the cave and into the snow-covered wasteland.

It doesn't take him long before he reaches the destination that was the goal of the party from Xaxtor. Cresting a rise he gazes down upon a massive army of orcs, trolls, goblins, and other foul creatures gathered around a black throbbing portal, which seems to suck the light from the surrounding area.

As the army spots Deramar, a great shout surges from them to bounce off the mountains.

"Ma'rel! Ma'rel! Ma'rel!"

V

Off in the distant sky, a speck appears, growing larger with each passing second as it heads towards them. Through her glassy, painfilled eyes, Dak'tari notices the sickly light of the sky reflecting upon the hard, smooth surface of the approaching figure riding upon the windless air. Growing ever larger, Dak'tari realizes that the light seems to bounce from only portions of the airborne creature while passing through other parts. Suddenly her eyes widen in surprise, forgetting her tortured agony, as she realizes the creature coming to fetch her to Gauntlar was none other than a draco-lich.

Twice the size of the fabled war galleys of Canthor and a hundred times more destructive and fearsome. Wheeling once overhead, its flickering shadow causes a strobe light effect to wash over the waiting captive and captors. Its massive frame thumps to the ground, sending a rippling beneath the feet of Dak'tari, as if two tectonic plates chose that moment to shift. Tucking its skeletal wings next to its hollow frame, the draco-lich turns its head (large enough to devour an elephant in one bite) to bear on Dak'tari.

"So this is the mortal that Gauntlar is so anxious to meet?" Its voice is as hollow and haunting as the lord of death's itself.

"Yes, this is the human," the mage replies, putting just a touch of emphasis on the last word, as his milky eyes quickly dart to Dak'tari.

"Good. Get on." The draco-lich orders. "The master awaits her."

"Get her on." Nephlyngard in turn orders the wraiths.

Thrashing, Dak'tari struggles against her invisible captors. Spitting in Nephlyngard's face, she screams. "You tra.."

The back of the mage's hand smacking her in the face cuts her off in mid-word. Clutching her by the throat he hisses near inaudibly. "Remember what I taught you human." Again the almost imperceptible emphasis on the word human.

Dak'tari's eyes narrow in anger, then start to widen in understanding. Nephlyngard's hand applies slight pressure on Dak'tari's throat cutting off the near give away. "Good, you understand," he hisses.

"The master is waiting," Mordigon says impatiently. "Stand back Nephlyngard." As soon as the mage is out of the way, the dracolich's giant gaping maw smashes into the ground enclosing Dak'tari in a toothy bone prison.

Extending its fleshless wings, it leaps into the air and flies off back into the direction from which it came. Through the slitted gaps in her gigantic enamel cell, Dak'tari spies the dreaded seat of power for Gauntlar. A ruined stone castle appears between the white stalactite and stalagmite teeth of Mordigon, lying in the midst of a putrid marsh full of bloated, decaying bodies moaning in torment. The four-round towers, which should be rising towards the sky, lie broken and smashed as if forgotten and unused for countless ages. Its' walls, covered in slime and mold, support the dangling, decomposing bodies of numerous poor souls trying vainly to shoo away the carrion birds picking away at their remaining flesh and organs. Placed on top of the walls stand rows of flayed skins, with the heads still attached, nailed to X-shaped supports, begging and pleading to deaf ears for release.

Landing in the courtyard, set within the center of the dilapidated chapel of pain, Mordigon vomits Dak'tari onto the ground; while Nephlyngard dismounts from the bony neck, where he was riding behind the skull.

Untangling herself from the marshy ground, wet, muddy, and dripping some kind of noxious goo, she rises to her feet. Two skeletal knights, in ancient and rusted armor, seize her arms in their bony grip; while four more surround her, and lead her into the castle entrance gaping wide like a festering wound.

Once inside the castle proper, Dak'tari is greeted by all forms of undead. Ghost and specters float aimlessly through walls ceilings and floor, bemoaning their lost past lives. Skeletons shamble about, seemingly on some mission that their brainless skulls' can not fathom. While zombies and ghouls feast on pieces of gray, rotted, maggot filled meat, torn from the bodies of those floating in the marsh.

Dak'tari, her escort, and Nephlyngard come to a stop before a towering set of wood doors, so rotted and worm-ridden that it seems they would crumble to dust at the slightest touch. When the leading knight lays a clawed hand upon the doors they swing open easily, and thump against the inner wall with a thunderous boom instead of collapsing into a splintered ruin.

Set in the center of the now exposed chamber, stands an enormous stone throne, carved into the likeness of a skull screaming in damnation. Surrounding the throne is a choir of twenty-four banshees, singing an ear singeing song of loss, loneliness, and despair.

Dak'tari's knees weaken in horror and awe as the god of death rises from the covering shadows of the skull-thrones tormented jaws.

Gauntlar stands over thirty feet tall, with maggots burrowing in and out of rotting flesh, which grow plump and gorged and then falls with the splat of an over-ripe tomato upon the slime-covered stone floor. Pieces of his rotting, diseased flesh peel away and flutter to the ground, like fragments of ancient marred parchment, exposing skull and bones beneath. Sores fester, pop, and ooze pus, that runs in rivulets down the entire length of his giant, disgusting frame, while the smell of rot, decay, and disease wafting over Dak'tari nearly cause her to vomit in its putrid intensity.

Towering above her Gauntlar glares down, upon the frail-looking female before him, with the same sickly, purple-glowing eyes possessed by the foggy skull and temple in Passail.

"So this is the mortal that destroyed Tha'gal and defiled my temple?" The anger and outrage in his chilling voice are as daunting as a tornado and twice as fierce. It washes over Dak'tari, freezing her to the marrow, leaving her stunned and terrified. Never in her life has she felt such fear, horror, and utter vulnerability swirling around like a nest of vipers in the pit of her stomach.

"Yes my lord," comes the voice of Nephlyngard, seemingly from a great distance.

"What have you done with Tha'gal's soul stone, mortal?" Gauntlar demands of Dak'tari.

The repeat of the word mortal and the mention of Tha'gal's name triggers a realization from deep within Dak'tari's frozen mind, causing wheels to thaw and slowly start to turn. She remembers the words of Tha'gal as she entered his sanctum 'you have no soul'. He had known she was different, he had known she was not wholly mortal. But how had the priest known and not his god? Then as more of the ice encasing her brain starts to melt away, it comes to her. His fury has blinded him. Somehow she must shove away from her fears, stoke the flames of his fury and stand before the furnace.

Slowly, hesitantly she begins speaking, and as each word is spoken she gains strength in seeing the desired effect. "I...I will.. never tell you. He was a pathetic excuse of a priest for a pathetic excuse of a god! But what do you expect with such worthless worshipers as Balsafar Ekthar. You should have heard him scream when I flayed him. Screamed as a babe snatched from the tit before full, he did. Ha! Ha! Ha!" She laughs in God's face.

Silence, complete and utter silence envelopes the room as the banshees cease their singing, and Gauntlar stands shocked that someone would dare speak to the god of death in such a manner.

Then Gauntlar erupts in a volcanic explosion of rage. Bellowing with all the fury of death denied, he sweeps out a massive, rotting, scar-covered hand and seizes Dak'tari, momentarily knocking the wind from her lungs. "NOW MORTAL, KNOW THE HORROR AND DESPAIR THAT IS GAUNTLAR!!!"

With his free hand, he rips off the rags that cover his emasculated chest. His rib cage splits at the sternum, exposing a withering mass of tortured souls trapped within the hollow cavity; slavering and yammering for the sweet fresh meat that is Dak'tari. Thrusting her into the horrid enclosure, the ribcage slams shut trapping her within. Dak'tari screams as a mydrid assortment of fanged mouths close upon her supple flesh. But as soon as the first drop of her demon blood touches them, they flare back as if burned; screaming in their pain and despair.

Instantly Gauntlar realizes his mistake. "No! No! It can't be!" It ejaculates in disbelief and horror, as he frantically tries to rip back open his ribcage, but it is too late.

Inside the cavity, Dak'tari transforms her suit into a mass of hooks and tentacles, then intertwines them around the rib bones; sealing the ribcage from the inside. As Gauntlar desperately tries to rip open his chest, Dak'tari begins the spell that will seal his doom. The spell Nephlyngard so laboriously taught her. The spell of resurrection.

A glowing ball of bluish-white light surrounds Dak'tari as she begins to chant, growing larger and brighter as she nears the completion. Outside the sheltered, self-imposed prison of the ribcage, Gauntlar screams in agony as the banshees wail in despair at the unforeseen predicament of their god.

Then Dak'tari utters the final word. The light is like a sun going super-nova, exploding outwards then collapsing in upon itself. Where Gauntlar once stood clawing at himself in vain, nothing remains except Dak'tari.

As the yellow, blue, green, red, and purple spots from the blinding light fade from her eyes she gazes about. Standing silently around her are the skeletal knights, the banshees, and Nephlyngard. Drawing her blade, which transforms into the katana (the first time it has transformed since she arrived on the plane of death), but nothing moves to attack her. Instead, they all bow down before her.

"What is going on?" She asks, astonished

"Don't you know my lord?" Says Nephlyngard reverently. "You have destroyed the previous ruler of death." He pauses, then goes on. "That means you have now taken on his mantle. You, Dak'tari, are the god of death!"

"Can it be?"

"Yes," comes the voice of Uthanor, caressing her. "The dead, the orcs, the trolls everything that Gauntlar held sway over, now serve you. But remember who you serve." He says sternly.

"You my love, always you," she replies, full of love for her lord.

"Good. You have done very well my child. I'm proud of you. Know this though, the other so-called gods are now aware of you and shall be prepared when you come for them." Then Uthanor is gone, leaving Dak'tari' god of death' to revel in her newfound powers.

Meanwhile, in Passail, the Temple of Gauntlar collapses in upon itself, leaving the stunned and confused priests to deal with the fact that their old god has been replaced by a new one.

The heavens shake and tremble as the remaining gods gasp in the realization that one of them has fallen and what that entails.

And through all of this Dak'tari laughs, while spinning in a circle, her arms thrown wide, as the dead await her commands.

THE END OF BOOK 1
PLOTS ARISING

PANTHEON OF TAMORA

MAXlMUS
- (Lawful good - Male) Ruler of the gods

Sphere of Influence - Maximus is the prime deity of all honor-bound knights, warriors, and good dragons.

Character Traits - Maximus is the defender of the weak and defenseless, though he will not tolerate a coward. He believes that if you are not at least willing to try and stand up for yourself, he has no use for you. His only weakness is his love and devotion to his wife Misatara. Who according to some of the other gods, "He would destroy the world if she asked while running her fingers through his fiery red beard."

Symbol - A golden dragon, its wings draped protectively around a flaming silver sword pointing upwards. Note: This is also the royal symbol for the kingdom of Reatha, who worship Maximus as their protector. Though he will deny playing favorites, he has been known to help Reatha in times of extreme trouble. I.E. Such as the time the dragons accidentally got loose to help Reatha in the "War of the Flame."

MISATARA
(Chaotic good - Female) Queen of the gods

Sphere of Influence - Misatara is the prime deity of non-evil spell casters.

Character Traits - Misatara is an extremely beautiful woman with ankle-length blonde hair. She is by far the most intelligent of the gods and along with being Maximus' wife, she is his chief counsel. She has a playful side, enjoying at times rearranging the stars into elaborate works of art and motion. Though this would normally play hell with the seafaring folk, who use the stars to sail by, the scenes never last more than a few minutes before returning to their normal positions in the sky. But during times of crisis, she is the most serious of the gods, setting aside her playful ways, and devoting herself completely to the task at hand.

Symbol - An arc of stars trailing behind a silver wand.

DISATARA
(Lawful evil - Female)

Sphere of Influence - Disatara is the prime deity of evil spell casters, evil dragons, and the dark elves.

Character Traits - Disatara is the identical twin of Misatara, but instead of blonde hair her's is jet black. If not for the perpetual scowl and burning hatred in her eyes, she would be Misatara's equal in beauty. She hates everything she can not control. She believes if she can not control it, then it is worthless and fair game for her destructive amusement. Along with her husband Lothar, they are constantly planning the overthrow of Maximus and Misatara.

Symbol - A shattering crystal ball, clutched within the claw of a black dragon.

LOTHAR
(Chaotic evil - Male)

Sphere of Influence - Lothar is the prime deity of thieves, assassins, and spies.

Character Traits - Lothar is the most sinister and conniving of the gods, he is also extremely intelligent. Preferring to work behind the scenes, he has the uncanny ability to take any situation, examine it from all angles, and determine all actions and counter-actions that would best enhance his chances of a favorable outcome.

Symbol - A skull with the jaw hanging open, with an open eye sitting in the mouth. A dagger pierces the top of the skull, extending through the eye and coming out of the bottom of the skull.

LEONESSA
- (Chaotic good - Female)

Sphere of Influence - Leonessa is the prime deity of nature, healers, light-elves, and fairy folk.

Character Traits - Leonessa has a deep love for all living things and all creatures that value life. Being the goddess of nature her moods and actions mimic the seasons and weather. She can go from being as sweet and calm as a spring afternoon, to the thunderous fury of a hurricane when angered. For this reason, she tends to be the chief deity of sailors. Always appearing as a female, her appearance does change according to her mood. She will appear as a human, elf, sprite, or even an animal depending on how she feels at the moment.

Symbol – A wreath made from golden oak leaves.

XAX

(Neutral – Dwarven Male)

Sphere of Influence – Xax is an extremely stout, dwarven male with a bald head and a waist-length red beard. He will appear wearing either a blacksmith's apron or a suit of shining plate mail armor with gold gilding, encrusted with gems. Xax loves three things in life: hard work, a good fight, and things that shine. Though not tempted by greed, he loves the pure beauty and perfection of mineral objects. Xax is the only brother of Maximus, reflected by the fact that they are the only two gods with the same fiery red hair. Though one is the ruler of the gods and the other lacking in height, there is nothing but mutual respect and admiration between the two. One of their favorite pastimes is to fight each other in a brawl. Most of the time these good-natured contests end with two equally exhausted gods with equally bloody faces. Next to Misatara, Xax is Maximus' closest adviser.

Symbol -A war-hammer slamming atop an anvil.

GAUNTLAR
- (Lawful evil - Male)

Sphere of Influence - Gauntlar is the prime deity of death, disease, orcs, trolls, goblins, and such.

Character Traits - Gauntlar appears as a rotting, diseased, rag-covered corpse. Due to his appearance and smell, the other gods shun him, but this does not bother him for he has no use for the other gods. He is too busy for them anyhow, with all the dying and sick on Tamora.

Symbol -A finger bone.

UTHANOR
(Pure evil - Non-gender)

Information - Known as the 'Nameless One.' He was cast down by the gods of Tamora over two thousand years ago when he first appeared and made a bid for control of Tamora. There is no other information concerning him. No one even knows where he came from.